No escape from the dungeon

A push from behind sent me through a thick wooden doorway and onto crumbling stairs leading down into the darkness. Before I could recover, the door closed and a bolt was thrust into position.

I stumbled up the steps, screaming, "Let me out! Let me out!" Terrified, I beat my hands against the door, but it stood firm.

Then I thought I heard the sound of laughter, and it was followed by the weight of a heavy, palpable silence. From somewhere far away came the occasional cawing of crows and rooks.

My fate was clear. I was a prisoner in a shallow subterranean cell of the ruined castle....

DOUBLE MASQUERADE

DULCIE HOLLYOCK

Harlequin Books

TORONTO • NEW YORK • LONDON
AMSTERDAM • PARIS • SYDNEY • HAMBURG
STOCKHOLM • ATHENS • TOKYO • MILAN

For my friend Helen Macgregor,
sometime Reader of the
Romantic Novelists' Association, London—
with love, appreciation and respect.

If the furze flowers twice
kissing has gone out of fashion.
—Old Irish saying

Published September 1985
ISBN 0-373-32006-X

CHAPTER ONE

The Eviction

I WOULD NEVER FORGET that morning. It would remain etched in my memory as long as I lived, to be recalled inexplicably by some association of events or to scare me in my dreams.

It was March 20, the beginning of spring and a dull day despite the season. I was an Irish peasant girl, eighteen years of age, tall, slim and vibrant. I had dark hair that fell to my waist when let loose from its bun shape and a creamy complexion that offset my blue eyes and dark lashes. People said I was pretty, and I hoped that I was, although the clothes I coveted were far beyond the means of my foster parents, and the famine had thinned not only my figure but my hair. I had been well educated by my foster father, who was an unfrocked priest, and domesticated by my foster mother, who believed that girls should be so. But the spring of 1848 and my own youth seemed inescapably shrouded in the misery of Ireland.

The potato crops that had promised well were green in the morning and black in the afternoon. The sun shone desultorily through the clouds as though loath to look on the wretchedness that for three years had plagued the land. The winding road of the village, thought to keep out evil spirits, could not deter the vicious bailiff's men.

We sat huddled together with our backs to the desolation. My foster mother, Anna McCabe, was keening softly, an apron over her head. Her young daughters, Bridget and Maureen, clung to her skirts as I tried to find words of comfort that would not come. And then our neighbor, Rose Mullarkey, and her son, Billy, a stripling of about my age, crossed the road toward us. Anna tried to avoid them by pulling the apron closer over her head.

"Have you eaten?" the unthwarted Rose asked.

Anna loosened the apron and nodded dismally.

"I've never seen a quieter eviction. Here you are on the roadside, with never a protest out of your mouths. Others I could name screamed loudly, steepled in their hands and knelt on the ground as though the bailiff, high on his horse, were the Lord God Himself."

"My husband warned us to go quietly," Anna said, "and him no longer with us."

"Aye, deep in his grave from the famine fever. There's naught Henry McCabe can do for us now, and him used to shouting out against the Parliament across the sea that gives us naught for famine and starvation." Rose turned on her heel, and motioning to Billy, rasped out in a voice grown rough like a man's from calling the cows home through wind and sleet. "Get you going to find the priest. No more can we do, with unpaid rents and eviction around the corner for all of us."

Dully, I watched Rose retrace her steps to her cabin, then felt a twinge of discomfort on my face as Billy Mullarkey's bare feet kicked up the loose earth from the road in his haste to do his mother's bidding.

Anna, not immediately resuming her keening but watching their departure with lackluster eyes, murmured in my ear, "'Twas Billy Mullarkey I thought you might wed had things gone well, Hannah."

"Mama," I said, pressing her hand.

"How many years has the good Lord put breath in your body, mavourneen?"

"Eighteen this spring."

"When I was eighteen, my first child was coming—William that died." She rocked herself this way and that in misery. "Never you go forgetting William that died, nor the good virtue neither that I drummed into you."

"No, no," I cried, swallowing hard. But my voice held a sharp edge. "What are we going to do?" I blinked back the tears that started to my eyes but knew that for all our sakes I must not cry.

"Wait," Anna said. "Just wait." Her lips tightened, and her high cheekbones jutting out sharply from her shrunken face matched the gauntness of her big frame. She returned the apron to her head as though to muffle the clatter of a donkey cart newly arrived at the scene of eviction.

Turning and staring back at our cabin, I saw a man thrust his head suddenly through the thatched roof below which my own loft bedchamber had been. With dismay I watched him tear out a handful of thatch and throw it toward the cart. Then the bailiff bawled out at his men, who appeared in the doorway and emptied our household utensils in a heap on the ground. From this distance I could see the black iron caldron that my foster mother had used that very morning to boil the gruel for breakfast.

Bridget and Maureen stared aghast at their mother. But after a while they got used to her sobs and skipped to the road to play who could see Father O'Toole first. While they were shouting to each other and squabbling about who should run to him when he did appear, I saw him coming up the road in his carriage from the opposite direction that Billy Mullarkey had taken. I put my hand on my foster mother's arm. "Mama, the good father has come."

Anna McCabe peered through a hole in the apron. When she saw the carriages, she flicked the apron aside and crossed herself, then stood up tall and straight.

"May the holy saints be praised," she said, calling Bridget and Maureen to her.

But to my astonishment it was not Father O'Toole who drew rein. The driver of the carriage was a stranger. His wide-brimmed hat sat low on his forehead, and he scarcely glanced at us as he spoke in a crisp, haughty voice. "Come. Which one is it?"

Bewildered, I looked at my foster mother, who avoided my eye.

"'Tis the best I can do for you," she mumbled, fidgeting, no longer standing tall and straight.

"Mama, what is it?" I cried, a chillness overcoming me.

"Two children and an adult are enough and more to burden my sister up Donegal way." She plunged her hand into the depths of her apron pocket and drew out a gold locket on a chain, which she thrust into my hands. Surprised, I looked into her face, but despite her tears, her eyes were blank. Wordlessly, almost surreptitiously, I slipped the locket into the pocket of my ragged gown. There was no time to look at it, but I could tell by the feel of it that this locket was uncommonly large, compared with those I had seen ladies wearing in town.

"Which one?" the stranger repeated with more impatience. The horse's head reared. It seemed as if the carriage were about to take off and disappear down the road.

Anna McCabe pushed me forward. I felt her lips on my cheek, her whisper in my ear. "Be strong in your virtue, mavourneen. Never forget that a girl that's strong in her virtue is more to be prized than rubies."

Puzzled, I returned her kiss; then a second push sent me climbing into the gig. From the tail of my eye I saw Bridget and Maureen staring, wide-eyed and curious.

"Where is Hannah going?" Bridget asked enviously.

"With the gentleman," Anna replied.

"Are we going too?" Maureen's voice was high-pitched with excitement.

"Wave to your sister," Anna said, "and not another word from the two of you."

Dazed, I waved back at them. The stranger opened his purse and tossed a handful of coins onto the roadway.

"Mama!" I cried. "Mama!" But my voice was lost as he urged the horse forward. I sat beside him, my face puckered with emotion. I looked back at my family and saw Bridget and Maureen scrambling for the coins.

Anna's voice followed me. "More to be prized than rubies!" She did not heed the coins, which the little girls proffered and dropped into her pocket. Then I heard her keening, no longer softly but louder and louder as the carriage moved father away.

The sun went in, and clouds darkened the sky. I was alone. Forlorn, hurt and frightened, I wondered where life was leading me.

The stranger did not speak. His hands moved capably on the reins, and I noticed that they were strong hands, neither blistered nor callused from hard work in the fields. I raised my eyes to his face and saw, beneath the rim of his hat, a strong profile—straight nose, well-shaped lips and determined chin. His skin was browned, as though he had been living in a much hotter climate than that of Ireland. I judged him to be about thirty years old.

"Well, young woman, what impressions have you formed?" he asked suddenly in a mocking tone.

I flushed and looked away quickly without answering.

"Well?"

"Sir, I've no impressions beyond an ardent desire to know where I'm going."

He favored me with a sidelong glance, and I saw dark brows raised quizzically above dark eyes. "You speak well for a peasant girl."

"My foster father was not only a field worker," I informed him stiffly. "He was also an instructor in a hedge school."

"A hedge master. Indeed." Again the mocking lift of the eyebrows. "It surprises me that your speech should originate from a low-class, illicit school."

Despite my personal concern, I said somewhat heatedly, "My foster father didn't see the hedge schools as either low-class or illicit. He—he believed that the people of Ireland should be literate as well as nourished."

"Where is he now, pray?"

"Dead." Overcome by sudden emotion, I turned to him, almost fiercely. "Who *are* you?"

"That is of little consequence to you. I'll not see you again."

"Where are you taking me and why?"

"Your betters will inform you more explicitly than I."

"Am I going into service?"

"I've no idea."

"But I've a right to know. Why did my foster mother send me away?" For instinctively I knew that Anna McCabe had been waiting not for the priest but for this stranger.

"She cared enough for you not to see you starve on the roadside, as will probably happen to her and her children."

"God forbid." I pressed my hands together.

The clouds, gathering overhead, burst suddenly into a sharp downpour of rain that beat upon my shoulders and through my ragged cotton gown. My companion glanced at me once or twice, but I stared ahead and folded my arms across my bosom. After a few minutes had passed, he said, ''Put the buggy rug about your shoulders. Otherwise, in that thin gown, you'll catch your death of cold.''

Without looking at him, I groped for the rug on the seat between us, but in my nervous haste I felt it slipping to the floor. As I bent down to retrieve it, he forestalled me, and, gathering the reins in one hand, placed the rug about my shoulders with the other. I said nothing, merely sat there and hoped that the rain would cease.

We left the road and turned into a winding byroad edged with rocks, furze and rhododendrons, which led us into the face of the wind. I could smell the seaweed and saw the waves of the Atlantic Ocean breaking along the rocky coastline. I felt a mounting excitement, all the more breathtaking because it was unexpected. My fear vanished as well as my embarrassment. After the journey along unknown roads, I suddenly knew where I was.

He looked at me with sardonic amusement, as though he sensed my pent-up emotions. ''So you do know where you're going,'' he observed.

''I do now,'' I said. Any thought that my foster mother had betrayed me into the hands of this stranger passed swiftly from my mind. In the dire straits of our circumstances, she had done what she could for me. Somehow she had contrived to send me back to Balaleigh.

Although my foster parents were lowly Irish peasants, I had always been proud that I was born at the

Big House, Balaleigh. There my mother had been lady's maid to the old countess. She had been seven months gone with child when, unexpectedly, the pains had seized her in the bedchamber of the countess's granddaughter, Lady Berenice, who had been breakfasting in the great four-poster bed. In anguish, my mother had made for the adjoining dressing room, and Lady Berenice had been obliged to pull frantically at the bell sash. On that first Thursday of the month, the house had been almost empty, with the inmates gathered on the Balaleigh common for the meet and the servants agog with curiosity at the basement windows.

When help had eventually come, it had been too late to move my mother. There, amid the glitter of Lady Berenice's toilet table and the fine silk and brocade gowns hanging in the closet, I had been born. I had never known my parents. My mother had died at my birth; no mention had ever been made of my father, and as I grew up, I had learned to accept my illegitimacy with a certain resignation. The first seven years of my life had been spent at Balaleigh, but when Lady Berenice had died prematurely, the old countess had sent me to live with the McCabes, who became my foster parents. As time went by, I forgot my early years; but now, as I saw the great gray house standing by the sea, memory encircled it with a kind of magic.

The stranger veered the carriage away from the byroad and toward a high stone wall. Tall iron gates were opened by the lodgekeeper, who touched his forelock respectfully as we passed through. We rounded a park of chestnut, beech and yew trees behind which I caught partial glimpses of the house. Then, suddenly it appeared before me, just as I remember it—a massive gray structure with thick stone walls and four gray towers at each corner of the battlement roof. It had the appearance of a fortress. I knew the old castle ruins were farther back, but the front of the house, with its narrow mullioned windows that let in the light through vertical bars and its oak entrance door that was reinforced by studded iron hinges, fulfilled the cold austerity of a stronghold. Neither the budding garden nor the fountain splashing playfully could soften this impression.

I had not expected the stranger to stop at the massive front doorway. Rather, I thought the kitchen quarters would be my destination. But he alighted with athletic agility, tethered the horse to the hitching post and sounded the harp-shaped door knocker, which I heard echoing through the interior. I followed, my heart beating painfully. I was sure that at any moment I would be ordered to the back of the house. I knew that a disheveled young woman in ragged clothing was not a fit person to be admitted through the threshold of the dwelling place of the earls of Balaleigh.

But my forebodings were fruitless. A middle-aged housekeeper, dangling a bunch of keys at her waist and wearing a tightly bodiced, full-skirted gown that matched the gray cap on her graying hair, curtsied to my companion. Standing to one side of the door, she beckoned me into the entrance hall. None of us spoke, and this omission somewhat reassured me. No questions were asked. I was expected.

CHAPTER TWO

Hipbath

I SOON LEARNED that being expected at Balaleigh was a very different matter from being welcomed. Without wasting any time, the gentleman disappeared down the hall, and I was left alone with the housekeeper.

"So you've come back," she rasped at me. I started at the hostility of her voice, racking my brains and searching my memory. "Mrs. Rundle!" I gasped, eyeing her circumspectly. She was much older than I remembered, slower in movement, more dignified in appearance, but certainly no less formidable.

"What you're up to I don't know," she went on disagreeably, "but you always were a sly one, worming your way in where you weren't wanted."

"I've been brought here," I protested indignantly.

"Doubtless. Otherwise you would never have been admitted through the front door. Stand here and don't start prying while I see what is to be done with you."

Leaving me in the dimly lit hall, she crossed the parquet floor and opened a carved oak door, which she left ajar. I heard subdued voices, and turning my

back to their sound, found myself staring at a portrait of a fine old lady that I remembered as that of the
countess of Balaleigh. She was attired in a gray gown
brocaded with multicolored silks and gold and silver
thread. The fitted bodice, pointed waistline and
flounced lace sleeves magnificently offset the auto-
cratic demeanor of a self-willed woman. I was not sure
if the countess was still alive, but the eyes, cold and
steadfast, dominated the hall. I moved uneasily, for
they seemed not only to pierce my own but to follow
me wherever I turned.

Not wishing to be mesmerized, I concentrated my
attention on the great marble mantelpiece, above
which hung the huge antlers of a deer. A fire, burning
in the grate, gave out little warmth. Two ornate hall
chairs and a plainer bench were pushed back against
the wall, but as I had not been invited to sit down, I
remained standing. Shivering in the cold, I waited for
Mrs. Rundle to return.

She was not gone long. She appeared in the doorway and, with a set expression, motioned me inside.
The room was lined with leather-bound volumes on
carved shelves and furnished with heavy leather arm-
chairs. A large window overlooked the park. In one of
the chairs sat a woman whom I recognized immediately. As a child, I had heard her referred to as the
"master's mistress," a phrase I did not understand,
for like everyone else, I knew that Mr. Scott-Ryan, the
master of Balaleigh, was a widower. Now, looking at
her with renewed curiosity, I heard Mrs. Rundle address her as Mrs. Scott-Ryan.

Her eyes traveled over my ragged appearance, and she drew a blue cashmere shawl more closely about her shoulders, as though the sight of me chilled her. I curtsied, taking in her dark silk gown with its high neckline and rows of gleaming pearls. She did not speak. Despite my nervousness and weakness, arising from lack of food, I felt my spirits rising. I would not be overawed.

"Would you kindly tell me, ma'am, why I'm here?" I asked.

Looking above my head, Mrs. Scott-Ryan ignored my remark.

"Speak only when you're spoken to," Mrs. Rundle snapped.

I stood my ground. "Surely I've a right to know." Neither woman replied. Then I heard Mrs. Scott-Ryan order the housekeeper to show me to my room.

Mrs. Rundle appeared at a loss. "Which room, ma'am?"

"The blue bedchamber."

"The blue bedchamber!" Mrs. Rundle gasped. I felt my heart fluttering, for I new that this bedchamber was reserved for very important personages.

"The master's orders," Mrs. Scott-Ryan explained. "And for goodness' sake, Mrs. Rundle, see that she wears something decent for dinner."

"Is she to dine at table, ma'am?"

"Precisely."

Mrs. Rundle's pursed lips conveyed her disapproval. Mrs. Scott-Ryan sighed and leaned back helplessly against the padded leather chair, her fingers beating a tattoo against its arm.

"Very well, ma'am. Thank you, ma'am." Mrs. Rundle turned to me irritably. "Well, don't stand there. Curtsy to the lady and be thankful there's room for you under this roof."

I curtsied, but it was like doing so to a wax effigy. Mrs. Scott-Ryan sat lifelessly, with closed eyes. Only the tattoo of her fingers on the arm of the chair signified that she still breathed.

"Up the stairs with you." Mrs. Rundle pushed me forward out of the library and across the hall to the great oak staircase. Clapping her hands, she called "Katie! Katie!"

A young fair-haired girl in cap and apron, slightly older than I, emerged from the shadows of a passage leading from the hall. "Yes, ma'am," she said, eyeing me covertly.

"Tell the scullery maid to bring up a tub of hot water for a hipbath."

"Where to, ma'am?"

"The blue bedchamber, of course."

"The blue bedchamber, ma'am." Katie's voice registered unfeigned surprise as her eyes passed over my ragged gown.

"That's what I said." Mrs. Rundle turned to me with averted eyes. "Katie is your lady's maid."

I said nothing, conscious of her emphasis on the word "lady" but inwardly digesting a privilege I never believed would be mine.

Katie fidgeted. "Seeing that she's in the blue one, ma'am, what shall I call her?"

Mrs. Rundle's face fell. "I'd not thought of that. None of us had thought of it."

Katie giggled nervously. "She can't go nameless—not in the blue room."

"My name is Hannah McCabe," I said distantly.

"Miss Hannah?" Katie asked, eyeing the holes in my gown and the threadbare hem.

"Yes, indeed." In my ears, my voice sounded confident, but I fancied I saw the same contempt on the housekeeper's face that I had noticed on Mrs. Scott-Ryan's. However, I was not contradicted.

Katie disappeared. I could hear her speaking to someone farther down the dark passage and fancied I heard a smothered giggle. She returned almost immediately and followed Mrs. Rundle and me as we ascended the stairway with its carved oak newels, red carpeted stairs and shining brass stair rods.

At the first-story landing, Mrs. Rundle unlocked a small gate with a key she selected from the ring dangling at her waist. I followed her along a passage that I knew led to the blue bedroom. Behind me was Katie. At the bedchamber door, Mrs. Rundle stood aside to allow me to enter. Somewhat nervously, I hesitated to cross the threshold, and Katie, not expecting me to pause, trod on and tore the hem of my skirt.

"Sakes alive!" she gasped. "I'm sorry, miss."

"It tears easily," I said, my face reddening.

Mrs. Rundle eyed me angrily. "Kindly remember, miss, that you're here at the master's order. Endeavor to comport yourself as a lady should. You're no longer a peasant."

"I've been living like a peasant," I flashed back.

"Do you mean to imply that you're not a peasant?"

"Peasants are not ordinarily brought to the Big House and given a bedchamber like this. Why am I here?"

"To mind your own business. Now take off those filthy rags and prepare for your bath. Katie, will you tell Mrs. Kelly to burn the clothes?"

"Yes, ma'am," Katie said, bobbing.

"Dinner is served at seven sharp," Mrs. Rundle went on, speaking like Mrs. Scott-Ryan, not to me but over my head. "See that you're punctual." She addressed Katie in a low voice and left the room with a rustling movement of her skirt.

A scared-looking chambermaid whom Katie called Mary arrived, weighed down by a tub of hot water, which she emptied into a hipbath at the side of the bed. Made of enameled tin, the bath was oval shaped and had an inclined semicircular back.

"Undress, miss," Katie said, not unkindly.

I waited until Mary had gone. Then I took off my gown, shift and underdrawers and put them on the blue quilted coverlet of the four-poster bed.

"Not there," Katie said quickly. She picked them up with her thumb and forefinger. "What about your shoes, miss?"

"These are the only ones I've got."

"There are others here, miss."

"But they might not fit."

"They will."

I took my shoes off, trying to hide the worn uppers. Katie seized them with her free hand, and holding both arms out, left the room.

Wondering whatever on earth I would do if another pair of shoes did not fit, I got into the bath and savored the luxury and comfort of warm water and sweet-smelling soap. Sitting back with my hips under the water, I looked about me. The room was furnished with a massive oak wardrobe, a four-poster bed with paneled head and tester, a washstand on which stood a blue china ewer and basin, and a dressing table fitted with drawers. The windows boasted blue brocade curtains and matching floor mat.

Katie returned. She stood silently in the doorway, surveying me. At last she observed, "My, miss, you're skinny."

Self-consciously, I folded my arms across my bosom.

"No offense meant, miss. Mrs. Kelly, the cook, will soon fatten you up." She handed me a huge bath towel. "Now, if you dry yourself, I'll sort out your clothes—your new clothes."

I frowned. "New clothes? Where did they come from?"

"Sometimes young ladies staying here left them behind. It's lucky for you that they did." She held up a shift, fine linen drawers and three petticoats, one of flannel and two of stiffly starched muslin. "You won't need corsets, miss, seeing you've nothing much to tighten in. The dress will fit snugly over what you've got." She opened the huge wardrobe and took out a blue worsted dress that matched the color of her eyes.

"Is that for me?" I asked, gasping.

"Who else, miss?"

"But why?"

"Miss, surely you know." Katie looked coy. When I shook my head, she went on. "In the kitchen they say Mr. Richard Ralston is looking for a wife."

"Mr. Ralston?"

"The gentleman who brought you here."

"How absurd," I said, overcome with surprise and adding quickly, "Gentlemen don't look to peasants for wives."

She dressed me with great care, and as there was nothing else I could do, I submitted, somewhat apprehensively. I felt the situation called for protest, but since I had no other clothes, common sense overrode my uneasiness. I was relieved that the kid shoes she produced fit me perfectly. But when she began to brush my hair, her hands dropped to her sides.

"I can't do it, miss. It's falling out at the roots."

"I know," I said sadly. For many months now I have envisaged myself with no hair at all.

"Never mind, I'll part it down the middle and let it fall over your shoulders—what is left of it." She worked dexterously. When she had finished, she asked me to walk across the room and turn around slowly. "A pretty picture, miss. That's what a lady's maid likes to see. A pretty picture." She handed me a looking glass.

Scarcely recognizing myself in it, I thanked her, but she told me ladies never thanked their maids and, with a slight bob, left me. A little later, Mary came in and carried away the dirty bathwater.

I went to the window and looked down at what I thought would be the park. Instead, I saw huge waves of the Atlantic breaking onto rocks at the base of the house. I noticed that all the windows were fastened securely. Otherwise in a storm, the sea could not fail to spray most of the room.

When the dinner gong sounded, I took a deep breath and made my way to the oak staircase. I felt nervous and ill at ease. What lay ahead of me? Katie was romancing, of course. Mr. Ralston had said he would not see me again. My reason for being here was for something other than that evoked by servants' gossip. A solution to this strange situation must surely await me at the dining table.

The dining room was next to the library, with oak doors opening from the rear of the hall. Nervously, I loitered outside, but when no one came, I decided to enter. Hesitantly, I opened the door and saw the inhabitants of Balaleigh already seated around a large oak table covered with a white damask cloth that offset gleaming silver, cutlery and sparking crystal.

At the head of the table sat Mr. Scott-Ryan, the master of the house, his table napkin tucked under his chin like a child. On his right was Mrs. Scott-Ryan; opposite her were her two sons, slightly younger than I, who, I soon learned, were home from Cambridge after the end of the Lent term in mid-March.

A parlor maid, wearing a dark dress, a white apron and a cap with trailing purple ribbons, was carrying hot dishes through a service door that opened from the rear kitchen.

I waited. I saw the parlor maid raise her eyebrows questioningly at Mrs. Scott-Ryan. But it was the master who nodded and bellowed, "Sit down, miss." Immediately, the maid escorted me to a place set at the foot of the table.

The young men eyed me curiously. Mrs. Scott-Ryan went on sipping her soup as though I had not appeared; the master drank his stoically. I noticed an empty place set beside Mrs. Scott-Ryan.

"A governess, would you say?" one young man asked of the other.

"Who's she about to govern?"

They sniggered together, but their quip fell upon unheeding ears. I began to eat my soup. Not even my uneasiness could detract from my desire for food. The meal consisted of spinach soup, an entrée of curried lobster, a forequarter of lamb, salad with vegetables and iced pudding.

Upon sampling the pudding, Mrs. Scott-Ryan beckoned to the parlor maid. "How many eggs were put in this Nesselrode, Ellen?"

"A good half dozen, ma'am."

"Is that what the recipe says?"

"One dozen, ma'am, but seeing things are as they are, it seemed too many."

"Aren't the hens laying?"

"They are, ma'am."

"Then no one in the kitchen has any reason to exercise judgment on a proven recipe."

"No, ma'am." Ellen lowered her eyes.

I froze. I seemed to see Anna trudging up Donegal way and her two little daughters, no longer skipping but lagging behind, tired and listless.

In a rustle of silk, Mrs. Scott-Ryan rose from the table. "I will speak to Mrs. Kelly about this in the morning." She inclined her head to the master, who was already making inroads into the whiskey decanter that Ellen had placed before him.

To the accompaniment of subdued tittering from the youths, I also rose, wondering uncertainly what I should do next. With relief I heard the master's voice. "Miss, I will speak to you in the library in fifteen minutes."

I curtsied and left the table. Once in the hall, I felt decidedly chilly despite the peat fire still smoldering in the hall grate. Not sure of my next move, I somewhat hesitantly entered the library. I felt the warmth of a fire from the rear fireplace but did not advance toward it. Instead, I settled myself on one of the dark leather chairs as comfortably as I dared. In the light from the oil lamps, the heavy furniture cast gloomy shadows. After sitting there for some time, I heard subdued voices at the doorway.

"The girl's here to stay," the master said. "I want no more of this nonsense, do you understand?"

Not wishing to eavesdrop, I half rose in my chair, but the exit was blocked, and I sat back, stiff and uncomfortable.

"You seem to forget," Mrs. Scott-Ryan said, "that I've given you two sons." The scent of her expensive perfume wafted inside the library.

"What use are they to me?"

"You should have thought of that and married me."

"Impossible. You know that. My wife, Lady Berenice, was still living when those two were born."

"You should marry me now."

He did not reply. Mrs. Scott-Ryan began to sob. "If you've brought her here as your mistress, I shall leave."

Shocked, I dug my elbows into my sides and heard his guffaw. "Don't tell me you're jealous of that skinny little thing." He walked into the library toward the fire. I saw her hesitate at the doorway, then turn away.

I made my presence felt by standing up.

"Ah, there you are," he said, turning.

"You wish to speak to me," I replied stonily.

"Indeed, yes." He helped himself to a pinch of snuff. "What have you to say for yourself?"

"I feel an explanation is my due."

"Your due? Since when have peasants commanded rights?

"I did not ask to come here."

He grunted. "I sent for you became Anna McCabe needed some relief. One less mouth to feed."

"You evicted her," I reminded him.

He ignored me. "A foolhardy plan to walk to Donegal. Only a miracle will save them all from starvation."

He sounded concerned, but I mistrusted him. "What else was she to do?"

He shrugged, toying with his snuff.

I more than mistrusted him. I disliked him. I remembered that when I was a child, he had cuffed me across the ears because I had sticky hands when he sat me on his knee. Now I saw the same crudity cloaked beneath the apparent fastidiousness of his white silk cravat, light-colored trousers and darker coat with a curved waistline that fitted ill on his thickset figure. His hands were coarse, the fingers small and stubby, although the nails were immaculately kept.

"Do you remember me?" he asked.

"It matters little whether I do or not. You had no great liking for me."

"You misjudge me, my girl. But then you always were an impetuous child."

"Why am I here?" I cried. "Why these fine clothes and a bedchamber fit for a princess while all the time your family ignores me?"

"You're allowing your imagination to run away with you."

"What rubbish! If you refuse to answer me, I'll seek information elsewhere."

"Where, pray?"

"In the kitchen," I said. "Servants know more of what goes on in a house than their betters."

He ran his eyes up and down my thin figure. "Did you enjoy your meal?"

I nodded, avoiding his eye.

"There will be plenty more if you behave yourself. I don't expect you to go tittle-tattling to the kitchen. In fact, I positively forbid it."

My tone became more conciliatory. "Please tell me why I'm here."

"To oblige your foster mother. Anna McCabe was a good servant to my wife, Lady Berenice. Do you remember her?"

"Yes."

"Later on, you will have duties to perform. Until then, enjoy your leisure."

"What kind of duties?" I asked.

"Your foster mother told you nothing?"

"Nothing."

"Then please allow the matter to lie."

"How can I when I don't know what is happening to me? If you had any heart at all—" But footsteps over the parquet floor interrupted my bravado. With a sudden lurch of my heart, I saw Mr. Richard Ralston join us. he nodded to the master and regarded me with surprise.

"I brought a ragged urchin," he murmured. "Now it appears you're a beauty."

I curtsied, suddenly dumbfounded. He was handsome, less dandified than the master in his dark jacket, tan trousers and plastron cravat, but conveyed more masculine strength. His face, like the master's, was clean-shaven, revealing a mouth less sensual and more determined.

Silently, I stared at him, trying to judge if he were friend or foe.

"Come," he said with some amusement, "you had plenty to say for yourself in the carriage."

"Sir," I replied, "subsequent events have been— rather sprung upon me."

"Indeed!" He lifted his eyebrows quizzically. "Young lady, your speech is not of the hedge schools. It is of London."

"I had an English nanny," I murmured, lowering my eyes.

"An English nanny for an Irish peasant girl?"

"Sir, I lived here for the first seven years of my life."

"Egad! Do you intend to spend the rest of your life here?"

I raised my eyes to his. "I've no idea."

Surprisingly, he patted my hand. Then he turned to the master, and they stood together with their backs to the fire, regarding me in silence. Self-consciously, I curtsied and fled.

On the way upstairs to my bedchamber, I saw the portrait of Lady Berenice, the master's dead wife. I remembered that it used to hang in the library, half hidden by the gloom, but here, on the great stairway, it dominated its surroundings. I paused to look at the oval-shaped face, at the fair hair dressed high on the head and supporting three tall feathers. Despite the elegance and grandeur of her rich white court dress, Lady Berenice was wearing no jewels. Her throat, rising above the low-cut neckline, was bare.

With a sudden quick intake of breath, I remembered the locket that Anna McCabe had handed to me. I clutched my throat in consternation. What had I done with it?

CHAPTER THREE

The Parapet

I RUSHED UPSTAIRS and burst into the blue bedchamber in a panic. The fire was burning in the grate. The oil lamp had been dimmed and the bedclothes turned down. I sat on a small oak chair and tried to think.

What had I done with the locket when Anna McCabe had given it to me? I had put it in the pocket of my gown. I had not looked at it. The moment had not seemed opportune. I had counted on looking at it later. The pocket was deep, and despite the ragged state of my gown, had no holes so the locket could not have fallen out. It must still be there. The horror of the situation dawned on me with frightening reality. Katie had taken the gown downstairs for Mrs. Kelly to burn. Was it even now being consumed by flames? Could a golden locket withstand the heat of the furnace?

I thought I would go mad with sorry. I tried to plan my course of action but could not. Instead, I busied myself with my toilet and was partially undressed when Katie entered the room.

"I'm sorry, miss. I was with Mrs. Scott-Ryan. I didn't know you'd come up."

"Katie..." I tried to speak, but my pent-up emotions strangled my voice in my throat.

"Yes, miss?" Katie picked up the hairbrush and gently parted my hair.

I managed to gasp. "What happened to my gown?"

"The old one, miss?"

"Yes."

"Mrs. Kelly's got it. She said she'd pitch it into the furnace in the morning."

"Where is it now?"

"Lawks, miss, how should I know? I saw old Dan feeding up the king. We call the furnace that, you know, after King James the Second, who got so badly beaten in the wars."

"Who is Dan?"

"The man-of-all-work."

"Has he burned it?"

"He could have. It was lying there on the heap. But why, miss? You're well rid of that ragged old thing."

"I left something in the pocket—something important."

"May I ask what, miss?"

"A locket," I said. "A golden locket."

"My, a golden locket in that gown!"

"Katie," I pleaded, "go down and see if the gown is still lying there on the heap. Look in the pocket."

"It's late, miss. The back door's locked."

"Can't you open it?"

"I expect so, miss."

"Please," I entreated her, feeling more like a frightened peasant than a princess in a gilded cage.

"Surely, miss, but I can't promise anything."

Alone in the bedchamber, I clambered miserably between the cool white sheets. But the luxury of the warm blankets, the soft pillow and the featherweight eiderdown brought me no comfort.

Katie returned shortly.

"Well?" I asked.

"Nothing, miss. But Ellen says Mrs. Kelly put the gown in the closet."

"I thought you said it was on the heap."

"No, miss. Ellen said it was in the closet." She avoided my eye. "I made a mistake. I must have seen something else."

"Did you tell Ellen about the locket?"

"Rather. Real surprised she was that you had a locket. She said she will look in the morning when Mrs. Kelly opens the closet door."

I closed my eyes and leaned back against the pillows. I did not believe I would ever see the locket again. Why had Anna McCabe given it to me? How had it come into her possession? Why should it concern me?

When Katie had gone, I tried to sleep. My heart was pounding in my chest. The events of the day raced through my brain, keeping me awake. I tossed on the huge bed. If the closet were locked, it was useless for me to go downstairs to search for the gown. I would have to wait until morning. My inability to act tortured me nearly to the screeching point, and despair racked my frame. Then, miraculously, I slept.

In the morning I was awakened by Katie standing in the doorway and staring at me with large, worried eyes.

"It's gone, miss. The locket's gone. Mrs. Kelly burned the dress last night. Dan is cleaning out the furnace, but he can't find any locket."

"Someone has got it," I moaned. "It wouldn't burn so easily."

"I'm sure I don't know, miss," Katie said, and went about the business of dressing me. But the novelty of the performance brought me no joy. Even the poplin gown she slipped over my head failed to arouse me. One thing was paramount in my mind. Anna had given me the locket for a purpose and my negligence had thwarted whatever design she had in mind.

What should I do? Other than ask the serving girls, I knew no other course was possible. The master was unapproachable, Mrs. Scott-Ryan was too inert, and Mrs. Rundle was too churlish. I dared not approach any of them. All would question my possession of the locket.

I breakfasted alone in the dining room. Ellen, in cap and apron, placed hot dishes on the sideboard.

"Help yourself, miss," she said. "Everyone does at breakfast." Then she murmured, "I'm sorry about your locket, miss."

Deeming that it might be wise to cloak undue eagerness about it, I helped myself to ham and poached eggs before asking, "Has anyone seen it?"

"No, miss. Real sorry everyone is in the kitchen."

"There must be some trace of it in the furnace."

"Dan could have shoveled it into the pit without noticing."

"How big is the pit?"

"Lawk-a-mussy, don't you go near the pit. You'd be buried alive."

I had finished my hot dish and was sipping white coffee from a breakfast cup when Mrs. Rundle bustled into the dining room. Instead of ignoring me, as I expected, she bore down upon me threateningly. "What's this I hear about a locket, my girl?"

"I—I've lost it," I replied, setting down my cup on the saucer.

"Stuff and nonsense. You're allowing your imagination to run away with you. No peasant owns a locket. The next thing you'll do is accuse someone of stealing it."

"My foster mother gave it to me," I said miserably.

She snorted. "Anna McCabe was no better than she ought to have been. Take care, miss. We want no peasant tricks in this household."

I opened my mouth to reply, but she flounced away before I could speak. Listlessly, I finished my coffee, afraid of her next move. Any time now I could expect to be summoned by the master. I dreaded the inroads into my privacy that he would endeavor to force upon me.

My thoughts were diverted by the entrance of Richard Ralston. Dressed in a dark blue jacket offset by a white silk cravat and light gray trousers, he projected a breath of fresh air by the vigor of his personality. But my heart did not quicken as it had done the evening before. My mood was too downcast, and I did not know him well enough to hope that he could lighten it.

He helped himself to the dishes on the sideboard, sat down next to me and unfolded his napkin. "Well?" he asked. "What has the princess to say for herself this morning?"

My voice was dull. "I'm no princess, and well you know it."

He lifted his eyebrows. "Shall I call you a peasant instead?"

"Call me what you like," I said ungraciously.

He attacked his porridge. "Has something upset you? Surely I have not been remiss."

"You have not."

"Then what is it?"

"Nothing." I turned my face away, having no wish to discuss my predicament with him.

"I was going to bid you the top of the morning."

"Pray, don't let me stop you."

He grimaced. "How can I when you look so glum?"

"My moods are no concern of yours."

"I dare say not. But a pleasant member of the opposite sex makes the day's work lighter—and more interesting."

I got up and left the table. He followed me, holding his napkin in his hand. "Hannah, what is the matter?"

"I've told you. Nothing."

His eyes narrowed as he considered me. "They do call you Hannah?"

"Yes."

"Where did you get a name like that?"

"It's an Irish rural name—common enough in these parts."

"Do you mind if I call you Hannah?"

"It matters little to me what you call me. I shan't see much of you."

"How can you be so sure?"

"You yourself said, in the gig, that you would never see me again. Or don't you recall the occasion?"

His smile was twisted. "That, my dear Hannah, was before I was aware of your standing in the household."

"Standing!" I eyed him, aghast. "What standing have I, pray?"

"You show a lack of servility that dissociates you from the evicted urchin I thought you might have been."

"So you were acting under orders. Then tell me why I've been brought here."

He resumed his seat before replying. "I take it Mr. Scott-Ryan has spoken to you."

"Yes."

"Has he not explained your position?"

"He told me to enjoy my leisure. How can I when he leaves me in the dark?" My voice sounded bitter.

"Enjoy each day as it comes," Richard Ralston said, helping himself to coffee. I felt his eyes on mine. I could have sworn that his lips parted in a smile. Was he sneering at me or merely being friendly? In my frustrated mood I was not sure. All I knew was that he was a stranger.

"Sir," I said with dignity, "your breakfast grows cold. Nor am I at all certain of your own position in this household."

He gave me a sidelong glance and a quick, unprovocative smile. "Perhaps the occupations of your leisure and my status could engross us at dinner this evening, Hannah."

I did not reply. But my mind was racing. Did he live here? Despite my own problem, I had to admit to myself that I was curious about him. His well-dressed appearance was that of a gentleman, while his aplomb and detachment of manner emphasized independence rather than involvement in cursory affairs.

Matching my mood to his, I sauntered out of the dining room. In the hall was a man-of-all-work; he was dressed in a smock and his bald head, glistening above gray hair, gave the appearance of a tonsure. He was carrying a bucket filled with peat to the small fire struggling for life in the huge fireplace.

"No locket, miss," he said when he saw me. "Old Dan never saw a locket."

"Did you look carefully?" I asked eagerly.

"Aye."

"Did you burn the gown?"

"Never saw a gown, miss."

"But you must have. An old ragged gown. The locket was in the pocket."

"No. Old Dan knows what he sees. He never saw a gown. An old bit of rag, maybe, but not a gown for the likes of you."

I cried out excitedly, "What did you do with it, Dan? The old bit of rag?"

He scratched his head. "If I remember rightly, miss, I burned it. On the other hand, my memory isn't what it used to be. I may have given it away." He closed one eye at me.

"Who did you give it to?"

"Can't remember, miss." Tenderly, almost lovingly, he fed peat onto the embers. "Who would want a dirty old bit of rag? Not me or you. And not the master or the master's mistress, for all that she calls herself Mrs. Scott-Ryan—which she's not. Mustn't waste my time, you know. If the fire goes out, the spirits take over."

"What rubbish are you talking?" I asked crossly, knowing even as I spoke that I could rely on nothing he said.

He put his finger to the side of is nose and whispered, "When the fire goes out, miss, someone is going to die, a member of the family. Do three turns around the old churchyard yonder at midnight and you'll see the devil. Let the fire go out, and the banshee will beat you to the graveyard."

"What utter nonsense," I said, and walked down the hall and through the open front door.

It was a cool, cloudy day, with a moderate wind from the sea. I followed a gravel path along an incline leading to the edge of a thick, gloomy forest of dark-leaved yew trees. Remembering Dan's words about the banshees in the graveyard, I shivered slightly and changed my course in the direction of the old castle ruins.

I had known those ruins since I was a child. The first inhabitant had been granted the ancient seat and elevated to the peerage by Charles the First. Now all that remained was a gray stone tower surrounded by rubble, grass and yellow furze. It rose high into the sky, no longer fulfilling its original purpose of a lookout. Time and erosion had eaten into the stonework, making the castle tower no more than a sorry heap of stones.

I walked back toward Balaleigh, which was separated from the ruins by a wide stone pavement. Dark clouds scuttled overhead; the hills, rising above the yew forest, castle tower and house, became a monotone of misty green enlivened only by a few patches of yellow furze in the hedgerows.

Certain that it would rain, I walked toward the western turret, which fronted the garden, and took shelter against its cold contour. A rising wind played about me and whistled through a long, narrow slit in the thick wall. I planted my feet firmly on the ground and felt heavy rain on my face. How long I stood there, sheltering at the foot of the turret, I did not know, but when the rain eased, I fancied I heard a hissing sound high above me. Surely no one had withstood the weather to peer down at my discomfiture from the stone-parapeted walk!

I raised my face in the direction of the sound, then heard a shattering thud at my feet. A huge stone had come hurtling down from above, missing me by inches. I crouched back against the wall, fearing a repetition, which fortunately did not come. Cautiously, I moved forward and crept out into the open. At a safe distance from falling stones, I protected my face with my hands and gazed upward. Tall, solid and silent, the turret stared back at me.

I heard a voice behind me and started suddenly.

"Quite a sharp downpour, was it not?" Richard Ralston was stamping his feet on a clearing in the grass and brushing raindrops from his greatcoat. "Did you get wet?"

"I almost got killed," I whispered.

"Killed?" He stared in amazement.

"A stone, that stone beside you—the big sharp one—fell down from the parapet while I was sheltering here."

He kicked the stone with his boot, but it was too heavy to be moved in a cursory fashion. "It looks too settled to have fallen recently."

"It was dropped from the parapet a few minutes ago, before the rain started. I—I heard hissing, then that—that stone—missed me by inches."

Richard turned his eyes from the stone to me. "Hissing, did you say?"

"Yes. Sharp but subdued."

"You heard it—from that height?" Deliberately, he gazed upward.

Overcome by his lack of concern, I began to sob. "Someone was trying to kill me." I covered my face with my hands.

"Come, come, Hannah. You're overreacting, you know. Who would stand on the parapet in this weather and at this hour of the morning to aim a stone at you? Did you tell anyone you were going out?"

"No, but someone must have seen me leave the house."

"Where did you walk?"

After I told him, he said, "You're allowing your imagination to run away with you. The weather often loosens stones, and they come hurtling down willynilly."

I was not convinced.

"Were you near the slit in the wall?" he asked.

"Yes."

"A fierce wind entering the slit can make a hissing sound. Doubtless that was what frightened you."

I stared hard at the stone. "It has a sharp edge. None of the other stones have such sharp edges. Someone deliberately threw it down."

Richard smiled wryly and, stopping, picked a spring of yellow furze from a bush growing nearby. "You're overwrought, Hannah. There was no undue danger; of that I'm sure. If a stone did fall from the parapet, it came down as a result of the elements and not from human force." He put his hand beneath my chin and lifted my face. I thought he was going to kiss me, and my heart leaped rapidly. But he merely said, "'May the links of friendship never rust.' These Irish sayings have more meaning than you realize. Remember that, Hannah, if real or imaginary trouble comes your way again. You know now whom to call upon." He shook the lingering raindrops from the furze, and placing the sprig in my hand, turned abruptly away from me.

CHAPTER FOUR

Thief

THE DAYS PASSED with a monotonous similarity. I did not find the locket, nor did anyone mention it. Almost bereft of companionship, I spent some lonely time wondering about myself and my future. I thought also of Anna McCabe, Bridget and Maureen and worried about their fate.

The climax of every day at Balaleigh was the evening meal in the dining room, with the fire lit and the oil lamps burning and Ellen waiting on the table for six. The master was always there, as were his sons, Philip and Eton. Mrs. Scott-Ryan was frequently absent on the pretext of a headache or a minor ailment. Richard Ralston was spasmodic in his appearances, but I, for want of better diversion, was also always there.

This evening, contrary to regular practice, the six of us were seated at our places, sipping game soup. A wood fire was burning fitfully in the grate, and the master glared at it once or twice. Ellen, seeing his irritation, unburdened the dishes she was carrying onto the sideboard and went to pick up the bellows.

Immediately, the master vented his wrath upon her. "Leave the bellows alone, girl. Your duties are to wait on your betters, not to concern yourself with the temperature of the room."

"Yes, sir." Nonplussed, Ellen bobbed and returned to the sideboard.

The master transferred his bulging eyes from Ellen to me. "You, miss, might give us the pleasure of your cooperation. Kindly rise and continue what the girl was beginning to do."

I put down my soup spoon in the bowl and regarded him questioningly. "I don't quite understand what you expect of me."

"I can't speak any plainer, my girl. I've asked you to blow up the fire—indeed, if need be, to fetch wood from the woodbox."

"The woodbox," I echoed, and saw Philip nudge Eton with his elbow.

"That is what I said."

"But the woodbox is probably outside the kitchen door."

"I've no idea where the woodbox is kept. All I want is a fire that burns."

"The wood is wet," Mrs. Scott-Ryan said. "No fire will burn with wet wood."

"All the more need for dry wood, then. While you're at the woodbox, girl, you might check on the amount of dry wood there."

I sat frozen in my seat.

"Move, girl. Move."

"I've no intention of moving."

"You will do as you're told, my fine lady."

"To all intents and purposes, you've made me a lady. If you wish me to be otherwise, inform me of your decision before I take my place again with your family—as a lady."

I heard the youths titter. Mrs. Scott-Ryan raised her eyebrows. I did not look at Richard Ralston, but from the corner of my eye I was aware that he had crossed the room and was using the bellows with vigor.

"Leave it," the master said. "Let the confounded thing go out. But you, miss, will not be excused so easily. Meet me in the library at the conclusion of the meal."

I felt like stamping from the room in a rage, but my good sense got the better of my impetuosity. Shamed and humiliated, yet with my chin held high, I finished the meal. No one spoke. The master had scarcely attacked his dessert when Mrs. Scott-Ryan rose and left the dining room. I folded my table napkin and followed at a respectable distance. But once in the hall, she glanced neither to the right nor the left, sweeping majestically up the great staircase.

Dejectedly I turned toward the library, wondering how long I would have to await the master's pleasure. In an attempt to boost my confidence, I sat down on a chair in front of the fire. The warmth comforted me, and I began to feel better.

He appeared sooner than I had expected and took up his usual position with his back to the fire. Following him, with a triumphant smile on her face, was Mrs. Rundle. I breathed deeply and was conscious that

Richard Ralston had also entered and was standing immediately behind my chair.

My heart thudded painfully. Was this some kind of inquisition? I clasped my hands on my lap and sat motionless, fearing to betray my agitation by any untoward movement.

The master moved to his desk and rummaged among a litter of papers. After a lengthy silence, he found what he was looking for and held it up. In the light from the oil lamp, it glinted gold in his hand.

I burst out, "The locket!"

"Is it yours?" he asked.

"Indeed, yes. It must be."

"Will you explain how this—this adornment came into your possession?"

"It is mine!" I cried indignantly.

"This locket," he said pompously, "belonged to my late wife, Lady Berenice."

"Thief!" Mrs. Rundle cried. "Prison is too good for you!"

"I was not aware," Richard Ralston interjected, "that this was a matter for the law."

The master cast a baleful look at Mrs. Rundle. "I will call upon you when I require your evidence. Miss, I'm asking you again. I want the truth, not evasions or lies. Can you explain how this came into your possession?"

"My foster mother gave it to me."

"Anna McCabe?"

"Yes."

"When?"

"The day I came here. We were waiting on the roadside, and when the gig appeared, she thrust the locket into my hand."

"Had you seen it before?"

"No."

He drummed his fingers on the side table. "Well, Mrs. Rundle?" He looked at the housekeeper.

"She's lying, I tell you. She's a thief."

"Can you prove it, madam?"

"A magistrate will, at the next assize, when the evidence is sifted. You're aware, sir, that she lived here years ago—before Lady Berenice died. That was when she stole the locket—when she and Anna McCabe were sent away after her ladyship died." She raised her hand and pointed an accusing finger at me. "It may be as she says. Anna McCabe may have given it to her on the day she returned here. She may have mislaid it. But it was she who stole it in the first place."

Richard's voice broke laconically into the discussion. "Surely she was little more than an infant."

"She was a child of seven."

He bowed to Mrs. Rundle. "I stand corrected, madam."

I tried to gather my wits. "Where was the locket found?"

The master's voice was like thunder. "What does that matter?"

"Was it found in the furnace?"

"How do I know? Where was it found, Mrs. Rundle?"

"In the pocket of the old gown she arrived in. Katie found it on the night it was missed."

"Why didn't Katie bring it to me—when she knew I'd lost it?" I demanded.

"La, la!" Mrs. Rundle sneered. "Katie brought it to me, as she should have done. I recognized it as the locket belonging to Lady Berenice. Hannah McCabe is dangerous, I tell you. It's a matter for the police constable, immediately."

The master turned to me. "Have you anything to say for yourself?"

"Only what I've already said. I'd never seen the locket until my foster mother handed it to me."

"You recognized it when I held it up."

"Only because the locket has been so much on my mind."

"It's time the police were called," Mrs. Rundle declared. "If you don't do it, I will." She glared defiantly at the master.

"One minute," Richard said. He was still standing at my elbow. "Is it absolutely necessary, Mrs. Rundle, for you to mention the police so often?"

"Whose side are you on?" she flared.

"I wish to see justice done. You forget it was I who brought the girl here at the request of Mr. Scott-Ryan. I seem to remember Anna McCabe's thrusting something into Hannah's hand that glinted gold."

"Are you prepared to swear to the magistrate that it was the locket?"

"Madam, why is it necessary to swear to a magistrate?"

"The girl will be brought to trial as a thief—at the next assize."

"Have you any idea what that means, Mrs. Rundle?"

"It means that justice will be done."

"In these days, at the least, it means transportation to the other side of the world." He touched my arm. "I don't wish to alarm you, Hannah, but these things must be said."

"The law will give her just deserts, Mr. Ralston."

Scarcely able to believe the turn that the conversation had taken, I was brought back to reality by the master's booming voice. "There will be no intervention of the law, Mrs. Rundle. The matter will be settled here, at Balaleigh. If the girl stole the locket, we must make doubly sure that she will not persist in her undesirable ways. She needs punishment."

"Bread and water are too good for her," Mrs. Rundle sniffed.

"I didn't steal it," I said dully.

The master's voice vibrated his authority. "Miss, you will remain in solitary confinement for a week."

I gasped, then clenched and unclenched my hands. Had I heard the master correctly? I felt Richard's hand on my shoulder and heard his indignant protest. "You can't do this, sir!"

"I am lord of my own domain."

"Sir, you are out of your mind."

"No more than a master punishing a recalcitrant pupil."

"It was you who sent for me," I said, trying to gather my wits about me. "I would like to know why. The whole matter has been shrouded in secrecy ever since I arrived."

Mr. Scott-Ryan did not reply. He motioned to Mrs. Rundle and said, "Take her upstairs to her room, madam."

There was nothing else for me to do but follow the woman up the staircase. We passed the portrait of Lady Berenice, but I withdrew my eyes from it. At the top of the stairs I saw Mrs. Scott-Ryan standing at the open doorway of her room. Neither woman acknowledge the other, and the housekeeper and I reached the blue bedchamber.

Alone in the room, I paced fretfully to and fro, knowing that I had made enemies. Instinctively, I sensed an alliance between the two women that, to my overwrought mind, foreboded evil. "Why, why, why?" I cried aloud. But the only reply was the lashing of the waves below me on the stone walls of Balaleigh.

That night Katie did not come to undress me, but early the next morning, after a sleepless night, I saw her standing beside my bed.

"Shh!" She put her finger over her lips. "The master told me to take you for a walk before anyone rises. Put on something warm, Miss. These spring mornings can be cold."

Astonished, I asked, "Why does he want me to take an early-morning walk?"

Katie tittered. "He's probably sorry you're going to be cooped up in your room for a week."

"I don't believe it. That was his sentence." I sat on the side of the bed and looked at her accusingly. "You lied to me. Why didn't you bring my locket to me when you found it?"

"I wasn't sure it was yours." Katie's eyes avoided mine.

"Why weren't you sure? I told you where it was. You knew it was mine."

"I just couldn't believe a peasant girl like you would own such a lovely thing."

"You thought I stole it?"

"I thought Mrs. Rundle should know."

"Why, pray?"

"It was you who made the mistake, miss. When you found you'd lost the locket, you should have gone to her, not me. She's the housekeeper, the one in charge. She was bound to find out sooner or later, anyway, and then it would be all the worse for you." Katie lowered her voice almost confidentially. "Not a thing happens at Balaleigh that Mrs. Rundle doesn't know, and what she knows, the master knows—if she thinks it's good for him."

"A nice little family circle," I said. But my sarcasm was lost upon Katie.

"Hurry up, miss," she said impatiently. "The master wants you back here before the rising bell."

"Doesn't he want Mrs. Rundle to know?" Katie did not reply, but I persisted maliciously. "Of course, you'll be the one to tell Mrs. Rundle—unless you're more frightened of the master than of her."

Katie tossed her head. "I'm not frightened of either of them."

"I don't believe that, either," I said, standing up and dressing slowly while she stood at the doorway. Like a jailer guarding a prisoner, I thought. But I said no more, and when I was dressed, she told me to walk ahead of her down the stairs.

"On tiptoe," she added.

We crept along the kitchen passageway, through the kitchen and outside into the cool morning air. The mist was lifting from the hills, revealing a monotone of green interspersed with yellow furze. Shafts of light shone on the smooth surfaces of gray rocks. A pair of crows cawed from the ramparts of the house; a flock of rooks flew overhead. Skirting the yew forest, Katie led me across the pavement in the direction of the old castle ruins. The gray keep rose jaggedly into the sky, and I shivered in the surrounding loneliness.

"When you feel two shivers down your spine," Katie said, "you've found a spot where someone died eating grass. Don't eat grass, miss, if you run away. Better to face the wrath of the master."

"I've no intention of running away," I replied coldly.

Katie walked close to the keep; some of the ancient dungeons could be seen at ground level. She stood deftly aside and maneuvered me forward. "There you go, miss. In there." She gave me a push from behind.

Taken unawares, I fell forward through a thick wooden doorway onto crumbling stairs leading down into the darkness of a dungeon. Before I could recover myself, the door closed and a bolt was thrust into position.

"It's locked," Katie cried through the slit in the door. "No one can open the door except from the outside, and then only with a key. Do you hear me? The door's locked. Don't fret. You won't need to eat the lichens that grow on the walls. You'll get bread and water in the evenings—if the ghost doesn't get them first. Enjoy your solitude, miss. Remember, it's only for a week."

I stumbled up the steps, screaming, "Let me out! Let me out!" Terrified, I beat my hands against the door, but it stood firm.

Katie did not reply. I thought I heard her laugh and after that there was silence, with only the occasional cawing of the crows and rooks.

I was a prisoner in a shallow subterranean cell of the ruined castle.

CHAPTER FIVE

Phantom

AFTER A WHILE my eyes grew accustomed to the gloom, and I was able to grope my way about the cell. The stairs down which I had fallen turned sharply to the left. In their crumbling state it was impossible to descend them, and even if I had been able to, I would never have risked entering the abysmal pit to which they led.

I thought I heard water dripping. I remembered that the sea was not far distant, and I trembled at the thought of the rising tide flooding the cell. To my right, dilapidated stairs led upward to another level. I tried to ascend, but the eroded stone gave me no footing, and I found myself slipping back helplessly. Better to stay where I was than face unknown hazards.

But surely this was not the master's idea of solitude. He had ordered me to solitary confinement for a week, but he had not said where. I had thought to spend the week of my punishment in the loneliness of my room.

I glued my eyes to the slit in the door. Outside, the sun, shining on the rubble, disappeared suddenly, as though it had been blown out like a candle. The sky grew overcast, and then it began to rain. Although the cell was protected by an upper story, this obviously did not prevent water from dripping in.

Through the slit I could see Balaleigh. Across the wide pavement that connected the castle ruins with the house, I had a good view of the front garden, and the west tower from the parapet of which I thought the rock had come hurtling down. In the distance I could barely hear the clip-clop of horses' hooves. I held my breath and glued my eyes closer to the opening in the door. Was someone coming to rescue me?

But when the gig appeared, it stopped at the entrance. Some minutes later, after the rain had ceased, the master came out, accompanied by Richard Ralston. Behind them, old Dan was carrying two portmanteaux which he placed in the carriage. The two men climbed in, the coachman turned the horses, and the gig skirted the yew forest, soon to disappear from sight.

Did the master know where I was? Did Richard Ralston, despite his claim to friendship? If they knew, the callousness of their indifference hit me like a whip. But if they did not know, would they not naturally assume that I was doing my penance in the blue bedchamber? With all my heart I hoped that this was so.

I wondered if I would be missed. Katie and Mary were the only two who went to my bedchamber, and Mary, I knew, would do exactly as Katie told her. And what about Katie? Was she obeying Mrs. Rundle, Mrs. Scott-Ryan or both? I had sensed that the two women were in league with each other. Now it seemed they were contriving to get rid of me—Mrs. Scott-Ryan because she thought the master fancied me and Mrs. Rundle because she wished to please her mistress. Katie, as a lady's maid, would know where her interests lay.

In that case, no one would know my whereabouts. I would be classed as one more unfortunate victim of the famine. "Don't run away," Katie had said. Yet she had pushed me into the cell and locked the door!

I gritted my teeth. I would not run away—how could I? Nor would I try to escape. Unbeknownst to me, the master had agreed with Anna McCabe that I should be brought to Balaleigh. He would not want to rid himself of me. He was merely biding his time for I knew not what. This convinced me that he had no knowledge that I was a prisoner in the keep of the ruined castle.

I looked around the cell. The gloom was oppressive. I dragged one of the larger stones to the doorway so that I could sit down when I peered through the slit. Knowing that I would have to sleep in the mustiness and dampness of the ruin, I selected a dry corner near the door and scooped away the rubble with a thin, flat stone. I pulled two bigger stones to one end of my improvised bed to act as a headrest. I lay down and saw, through the gaps in the wall, that the sky was still gray-blue.

I could not sleep. I got up, stamped about the prison, then sat down on the stone. There was nothing to do but sit and watch and wait.

I thought I would go mad.

I felt hungry, but no food came. I went back to the corner and turned my face to the wall. I must have slept, for when I awoke, the cell was streaked with moonlight. At the foot of the door I saw a crust of soda bread and a mug of water. Someone, either Katie or Mary, had pushed the food and drink through a hole at the base of the door.

I ate and drank. Slightly appeased, I sat down at the opening. Intermittently, lights began to appear in the three-story house. As the evening wore on, they disappeared, and the great gray structure that was Balaleigh stood in darkness. But not quite so. I glued my eyes to the opening and shivered suddenly. High up in the west tower a faint light was gleaming. Who lived there, in a solitude that must surely match my own?

I watched, but my attention was diverted from the light to a sound that seemed to come up from the abysmal pit. With a dry mouth and bated breath, I listened. I heard a wheeze, then trudging footsteps. Someone was mounting the crumbling stairway to the cell, from which there was no exit except the bolted door!

My legs grew weak beneath me, but I forced myself to leave the spy hold. Backing along the wall, I reached the corner where I had slept. My heart was thumping with terror. I could not breathe. I clasped my hands over my bosom to quell the uncontrolled racing of my heart. I gritted my teeth for I knew I must not cry out. Hiding here in the gloom was my only protection.

The figure of an old, unkempt man emerged from the pit. From where he had come I did not know. His body was wrapped in a dark cloak; tawny hair rose wildly from his head; the clawlike fingers of his hands grasped at the wall for support. Once in the cell, he straightened himself and groped his way toward the door.

I thought I would faint from sheer fright and exhaustion. The door was locked. Neither of us could get out. Yet it appeared he was used to doing that. When the door refused to budge, he kicked it with his boot and pushed heavily with his shoulder. The door flew open, admitting moonlight and a cool breeze.

I crouched down but he did not look back. He stumbled out into the open, wheezing his way over the rubble and around the corner of the keep. I waited until he had disappeared. Then I walked swiftly through the door. How it had opened did not concern me. My only thought was escape. Keeping to the shadows, I moved across the pavement between the ruins and the house and made for the massive stone steps leading up to the heavy oak door.

As I expected, the door was locked. I ran past the east tower to the side path that led to the kitchen at the back of the house. Breathless, I pushed the kitchen door open and saw Katie sitting at the table, drinking a glass of milk.

She looked at me, unperturbed. "I thought you'd either died of fright or got out and run away."

"I had no intention of doing either." Deliberately, I reached for the glass of milk she had relinquished and regarded her accusingly. "You pushed me in there and locked the door."

"I was just going back to take another look. I was waiting until everyone was asleep. I'm sorry, miss. I unlocked the door when I brought the bread and water, but you didn't seem to be there. I thought you'd run away. I couldn't imagine how you'd got out.''

"I was asleep.''

"Honest, miss, I didn't mean any harm. Mrs. Rundle said to lure you into the keep while the master was away and let you out when he returned. When he didn't come back this evening, I knew I'd die of fright if I had to spend the night down there.'' She began to cry. "If Mrs. Rundle finds out I've let you out beforehand, she'll send me back to the workhouse.''

"The workhouse!'' I echoed.

"I'm here on the rounds, miss. We do the domestic rounds of all the big houses in the parish, and the master said I could stay if I behaved myself.''

But my mind was preoccupied with what she had said earlier. "Why did Mrs. Rundle ask you to do this?''

"To give you a fright—and to please the mistress. You'll learn, miss, if you stay here. But they'll ignore you, Mrs. Scott-Ryan and Mrs. Rundle, because they both know that the master has taken a fancy to you, skinny as you are. Mrs. Rundle thought you might run away. They both thought you would. They wanted you to. That's why they told me not to bolt the door.''

"But the door *was* bolted.''

"I bolted it because I thought you might change your mind and try to escape. No one survives out there on those famine-stricken roads.''

"How does Mrs. Rundle know I won't tell the master?''

"He wouldn't believe you. It's not worth the trouble. All Mrs. Rundle will say to him when he arrives back is that she's relented. He'll be relieved. All *he* wants is for you to be safe and sound."

"Why?" I interposed quickly.

Katie shrugged and did not reply.

After a while I asked, "What am I to do now?"

"Go to your room, miss. I'll come to you in the morning and dress you as usual. By then Mrs. Rundle will have seen the master, and all will be well. She's very clever, you know. They both want him—Mrs. Rundle and Mrs. Scott-Ryan, for all that she's borne him two sons. He doesn't want either of them—not now." She smiled as she poured herself another glass of milk.

Katie's disclosures were, to say the least, enlightening. But I was exhausted after my ordeal and only too glad to retire for the night. Katie did not accompany me. Officially, I was confined to solitude in my room; unofficially, in Mrs. Rundle's eyes, I had been abandoned in the keep. I would wait in my room until the master returned, and she would be none the wiser that I had gotten out before he actually came back. Although I did not trust Katie, I did not wish to blacken her in the eyes of Mrs. Rundle.

I awoke about eight o'clock the next morning and heard the clip-clop of horses' hooves on the pavement below. The master had returned. I had no way of knowing whether Richard Ralston was with him.

I slept fitfully until eleven o'clock, when Katie came to dress me. Mrs. Rundle, her keys jingling at her waist, followed her into the room.

"It's as I told you," Katie said to the housekeeper. "When I heard the master's gig this morning, I did what you told me. I sneaked across to the keep and told her to come out. We came back here and she's been sleeping ever since."

I was surprised at the plausibility and partial truth of Katie's explanation as to why I was back in my room. Mrs. Rundle looked at me dubiously but merely said, "You can consider yourself no longer under detention. Thanks to me, the master has relented." Snorting, she left the room.

Katie whispered gleefully, "She got around the master just as I said." I did not reply and was relieved when my toilet was finished.

I spent a lonely day in the library, seeing no one and diverting myself with *Punch* and Mr. Thackeray's new serial, *Vanity Fair*.

At dinner, the master ignored me, which I took as an omen that I would not be ordered upstairs. Mrs. Scott-Ryan seemed unaware of my presence. Ellen served me two helpings of cabinet pudding. Philip and Eton nudged each other and whispered together. Richard did not appear, nor did Mrs. Rundle enter the dining room on a domestic pretext.

The matter was ended. But was it? I had not been given back my locket, which I assumed Mr. Scott-Ryan still had in his possession. I supposed that, strictly speaking, he had a right to it unless Anna McCabe had obtained it by legal means.

Before retiring at night, I sat at the window, observing the west tower. The light did not appear, and I began to feel that I must have imagined it. But the reality was still too vivid for me to disillusion myself. The light in the tower and the phantom of the dungeon remained fresh in my memory. From then on, I kept a watchful eye on the servants of Balaleigh, but none presented the wild, unkempt appearance of the man I had seen. Who he was and why he had appeared in the keep were riddles still to be solved.

And then one night I saw a pale glow in the uppermost window of the tower, which was still slight when I retired. It occurred to me then that the fact of the light was no secret. Not only I but others as well must have seen it. I decided to bide my time. Not altogether trusting Katie, I kept my own counsel.

Uppermost in my mind was the reason for my residence at Balaleigh. But I hardly ever saw the master, Mrs. Scott-Ryan never spoke to me, and Mrs. Rundle ignored me.

When Richard returned, the vigor of his masculinity brought fresh life to the house. Every Thursday he rode to the meet, mounted on a thoroughbred gray and immaculately attired in a red coat, white cravat, dark silk top hat and gloves. When the prelude was held at Balaleigh, anticipation ran high with the arrival of the horse boxes in the private road opposite the house. It was pleasant to watch the ladies sitting sidesaddle, the skirts of their riding habits attached to the pommel, and the men looking impeccable in top hats and pink or black tailcoats; to see the stirrup cup passed around, the horses freshly clipped and plaited, the arrival and departure of the hounds; and to share the excitement of ruins snatched up, flurried greetings exchanged and the rampage over Balaleigh's acres in search of the fox.

I could not ride and was an onlooker only. When Richard offered me the use of a quiet gray, I refused, much to the scorn of Mrs. Scott-Ryan and Mrs. Rundle, who were watching. The master did not ride. It was left for Richard to do the honors for Balaleigh, which made me wonder just who and what he was. But there was no one I could ask, so I had to accept him at his own valuation, which was considerably high.

I had no knowledge of his other pursuits. He presented himself as a country gentleman on the Balaleigh estate, although, apart from occasional meets, it was not a social place. It offered no entertainment for such a desirable bachelor, but then Balaleigh was not his home. That I knew for certain. Nor was it the home of the master or Mrs. Scott-Ryan. From childhood I had known that it was the dwelling place of the old countess of Balaleigh.

It amazed me that no one ever mentioned her name, and I wondered what had become of her. Without soliciting information openly, I took advantage of an opportunity that presented itself one evening, after Katie had cleaned my tortoiseshell comb with a small brush and was wiping it with a cloth.

"You're very thorough," I observed.

"A lady's maid has to be, miss. The old countess always expected it. They say there never was a more demanding mistress."

"Is she still alive?" I asked casually. I knew I was on safe ground. Curiosity about the old lady could prejudice me in no one's eyes.

"One hundred and three years old, she'll be," Katie said, curling strands of hair around her forefinger with the comb. "It's amazing how your hair has grown, miss."

"Indeed, yes."

"The old countess always wears a wig. One hundred and three years old on her next birthday. Some say one hundred and seven. She was here in the Rebellion of Forty-five, when the family lived in the keep and the tower was a lookout for Jacobites."

"Is she still at Balaleigh?"

"Lawks-a-mussy, miss! What causes your interest?"

"I heard of her as a child."

"If you must know, she comes back to Balaleigh for her birthdays and lives in yonder tower. Not the ruined keep but the west tower, where nobody is allowed to go."

"Why not, pray?"

"Master's orders, and carried out to the letter by Mrs. Rundle."

"Does anyone ever see her?"

"Only on her birthday. They bring her down from the tower in a Bath chair attached to pulleys. Six stories down and her likely to fall any minute. Not that the master would let her fall. He's fond of the old countess."

"Who looks after her?"

"The master arranges that when she arrives. She doesn't like company, you know. She likes to be alone."

"Not all the time?"

"Miss, I've told you. The master sees that she is well looked after."

"If she likes to be alone, aren't they afraid she might die without anyone knowing?"

Katie shrugged. "If she did, the hall fire would go out. If one of the blood of Balaleigh dies, the fire goes out." Placidly, she went on curling my hair. I wanted to know more, but I did not wish to arouse her curiosity by appearing too probing.

Now that I knew there was no mystery about the light, its fascination lessened. However, I could not resist an interest in the tower itself, within whose heights the old lady was confined and from which I believed the stone that nearly killed me had fallen.

Richard, crossing the pavement between the garden front of Balaleigh and the rear of the old ruins after a day's hunting, caught me staring upward and stopped to greet me. "Does the old tower till obsess you, Hannah?"

"A little. But I never go too near."

He smiled. "Not afraid of another stone, are you?"

"No." I felt suddenly tongue-tied. What had I to say to a man of Richard Ralston's stature?

"It's the oldest part of the house," he said. "But it's not safe. For that reason Mr. Scott-Ryan forbids anyone to go near it."

I said carelessly, "I thought I saw a light in the upper window, but I may have fancied it."

He gave me a quick look. "To use that tower would be suicide. The outside structure is solid enough, but the stairs inside are crumbling." He walked along beside me as I began to move back to the house. "You have a vivid imagination, Hannah. First a falling stone—"

"Isn't that likely?"

"A falling stone, yes, but not one aimed to maim or kill. Now you claim to have seen a light in the upper chamber of an uninhabited tower." He stopped, and automatically I followed suit. He looked at me for a moment, then put his hand beneath my chin and raised my face to his. "You're having illusions about the moonlight, my dear. A full moon shining through the windows may give the illusion of a light."

I was unconvinced and saw that his eyes were teasing me. With a deft movement his arm went about my waist; his lips pressed lightly, then more forcibly, on my lips until his mouth savored mine. With a little cry I pulled myself sharply away.

His lips moved from my mouth to my ear. "Surely the yellow furze that crowns the hills has flowered twice this year." Ruefully, he withdrew his arm from my waist.

"What has the yellow furze to do with—with moonlight?" I receded from his close proximity.

He grimaced. "A young lady bred in these hills should know why."

"It never flowers twice," I said.

"Indeed, no. It never does. For an obnoxious weed, that's the only good thing about it, my dear. It never flowers twice." He paused, then raised his hat in an elegant gesture. "Good afternoon to you, Hannah."

He turned from me with a slow deliberation and walked with long strides toward the small gate that opened into the dense yew forest. Dazed, I watched his retreating figure disappear into the shadows of the trees. I put my hands to my lips, which still smarted from the pressure of his. With a quickening breath, I headed back to Balaleigh.

My mind was whirling not only from his kiss but from the two conflicting stories of the old countess's place of residence.

Whom was I to believe? Richard or Katie?

CHAPTER SIX

The Crumbling Stairs

THE DAYS WERE LONG, monotonous but uncomplicated. Devastation caused by the famine did not touch me at Balaleigh simply because I had little or no contact with the outside world.

Domestically, the house was under the control of Mrs. Rundle. Katie, Mrs. Kelly, Ellen, Mary, and old Dan, lived in the servants' quarters in the basement. Additional servants, when needed for occasions such as the Balaleigh meet, were engaged from the village and did not live in. The coachman, groom and stable-boy occupied quarters at the rear of the house near the stables.

Possibly as a result of the master's singular personality, entertainment, apart from the sporadic meet, was nonexistent. Neighbors did not call or leave cards, nor did the master or Mrs. Scott-Ryan visit their neighbors.

I knew that more people than ever before were suffering eviction from their cabins because they could not pay rent and that thousands were dying on the roadside from starvation. But I was not face-to-face with the situation and could assess it only by hearsay.

In the sheltered world of Balaleigh, I moved backward and forward like a caged bird. I was not one of the household, nor did I have, as yet, any idea why I was there. The master alone could enlighten me, but the master was never about.

The responsibility of running the estate seemed to be in the hands of Richard Ralston, whom I did not care to approach with a personal problem. He was far too confident and self-assured. Beneath his debonair exterior, I sensed he could be ruthless, too, which made me avoid him.

So each day when I was not out walking, I sat in the library, reading the latest installment of *Vanity Fair* from subscription copies of *Punch*. I buried myself in romantic novels by such writers as Frances Trollope, the countess of Blessington and Catherine Frances Gore. Many of the books depicted life in high society, which I failed to find in my seclusion at Balaleigh.

The library was seldom used by anyone in the house. But one afternoon, when I was curled deep in a leather armchair and reading voraciously, Mr. Scott-Ryan stomped into the room, followed by Richard.

"Where did you say you saw him?" the master barked.

Richard's voice, in contrast, was controlled and calm. "Making his way to the village."

"For what purpose? He has no money."

"I didn't press for details. My main concern, when I caught up with him, was to get him to come back. He's getting old, you know."

"Hmm." The master did not elaborate, and a long silence ensued. Guiltily, I huddled into the armchair, uncertain about declaring my presence to the two men in whose company I felt uneasy. Eavesdropping was abhorrent to me, but the thought of standing up and drawing attention to myself was even more distasteful. So I sat hidden in the huge chair, scarcely daring to breathe.

Just as I was beginning to wonder if Richard had silently vacated the room, the master asked, "When do you intend to leave?"

"In a few weeks."

"So soon. Have you taken a fancy to some young colonial woman?"

Richard laughed. "Egad, sir, there's no accounting for affairs of the heart." Then the banter left his voice. "What is engaging my attention at the moment is talk of the discovery of gold in New South Wales. Why not avail yourself of an opportunity that is known to only a very few?"

"Gold fever sends men mad." The master humphed. "Do you expect me to risk that—in a convict colony such as Australia?"

"Many will," Richard said, "when the secret is out."

The master grew excited and began to shout. "This famine will not last forever. Grain, *my* grain, is selling in large quantities—for a profit. When the blight goes, the peasants will eat and work again. I could make you my successor—will the estate to you."

Richard's voice was bland. "Sir, you are not the inheritor. You're an incumbent in this family by way of marriage only."

"Fiddle-faddle! Ally yourself to me and you'll lose nothing."

"I prefer making my own way."

"In the colonies. Bah!" The master coughed violently, and when he had recovered, I felt the draft from the open door. Richard had gone. Unfortunately, at that moment the book on my lap fell to the floor.

"Who is there?" the master thundered.

I rose to my feet and saw him seated at his writing desk.

"Come forward and show yourself," he commanded.

Red-faced, I obeyed.

"How long have you been here, miss?"

"I sit in the library every day," I babbled.

"For what reason, pray?"

"To pass away the time."

"To eavesdrop, you mean. Who gave you permission to sit here?"

"No one. But I must do something." My voice rose. Now that my guilt had come out into the open, I felt the need for self-assertion. I refused to be bullied or to remain passive forever. "I can't go on living here day after day with nothing to do. The only people I see are the servants."

"You weren't brought here to gossip with inferiors."

"Why *was* I brought here? Can you tell me that?"

Mr. Scott-Ryan beat a tattoo on the leather top of the desk. "Not to create a commotion, that is certain."

"I need to know."

He was silent.

"You said I would have certain duties."

"Eventually."

"Why can't I begin now?"

"The time is not yet ripe, nor are you ready." He rose heavily. "In this world, my girl, money is the hallmark—the chief hallmark—of success. Attach that to gentle birth and life presents no obstacles."

"I have neither," I protested, my mind whirling.

"No," he agreed. "You have neither. When I've proof that you can do a day's work circumspectly, I'll have more to say to you. Until then, bide your time." He inclined his head to me, and I knew the conversation was ended. There was nothing else to do but leave my book on the chair and go out into the hall.

It was late afternoon. Despite the peat fire and the sunlight slipping through the mullioned windows, I shivered. The stone walls were thick, making this the coldest part of Balaleigh.

I mounted the great staircase and stared down at the hall through the banisters. Had there ever been life here, real life, with gentlemen bowing and ladies curtsying, music playing, the dance quickening, eyes glowing softly in the light from oil lamps? I thought not. The hall was drafty, cold, austere. It was a place for ghosts, not love, life and laughter.

I reached the first story. Along the passage was my bedchamber and, farther down, the private apartments of the master, Mrs. Scott-Ryan and their sons, Philip and Eton.

I continued upward, along narrow stairs. The second story was musty, unused and lit only from thin, perpendicular slit windows. Most of the doors were shut, and those that remained open revealed unfurnished rooms.

I walked down a long corridor and reached a winding flight of stone stairs that led to the tower rooms. After deciding to go on, I immediately encountered difficulties. It was dark save for the light from the window slits. In some places the steps had completely disappeared. My feet sank into rubble, and I could not gain a footing. There was no handrail to which to cling.

I stopped and gazed upward with pounding heart. I knew now why the master had forbidden ascent, but I was determined to reach the top. For support, I worked my hands along the damp wall, which was covered spasmodically with lichen and moss.

I heard a hissing sound. "Use the other side," a laconic voice directed me. I looked up and saw a tall, dark figure and a wild mass of tawny hair. It was the phantom. He was standing at the top of the stairs, regarding me with scorn.

Did I dare to continue? But if I turned around and clambered down, in my agitation I would fall and he would pursue me, would push me headlong down the twisting apology of a stairway.

I decided to face him and moved to the other side of the stairs. With every step I took, I slipped back again, but I went on, inch by inch, persistently, crawling on my knees. At the top I would have slipped if I had not grasped the helping hand that the phantom held out to me. Its warmth gave me unexpected confidence, and I felt less afraid.

"Heave-ho!" he cried with gusto. "Heave-ho!"

With both hands he pulled me bodily upward and, breathless, I reached the safety of the landing and leaned against the wall for support. His crackling laugh rang out clearly. He was no phantom. He was flesh and blood.

"Didn't expect to see anyone, or did you?" His face leered at me.

"I—I—" But I could not speak. My words choked back in my throbbing throat.

"Master," he called. "Master. Come quick."

I trembled. Was the master here? How had he come? Had he willed himself wings and flown upward? Surely anything was possible in this ghostly place. Then I heard footsteps, and my heart pounded afresh. A figure appeared on the landing, but it was not, as I had feared, Mr. Scott-Ryan. It was Richard Ralston. I put my hands, dusty and smarting from gravel rash, over my face and wept.

He picked me up, carried me through a doorway and set me down on a chair. I clutched at him with relief, then sobbed again at the painful contact of my hands on his coarse tweed jacket.

"A glass of water," he commanded the man. The water appeared with surprising speed, and Richard held the glass to my lips and said, "There, you'll feel better in a minute."

The hysteria passed in a few moments, and I felt my pride returning. "I—I'm sorry," I sputtered. "I—I went exploring. I didn't expect to see him—or you."

"Exploring!" One eyebrow rose quizzically. "What did you expect to find here?"

"I don't know."

"Yes, you do." His hand was under my chin. He raised my face so that he could look deep into my eyes. "Come along, Hannah. Be honest with yourself—and me. Whom did you expect to find?"

"The old countess of Balaleigh," I replied miserably.

"He-he-he," the old man sniggered. "He-he-he." But his mirth died quickly at the sight of Richard's heavy frown, and he sniffled into his handkerchief.

"Why in the name of fortune were you looking for her?" Richard demanded. "Is she a friend of yours?"

"No." I bit my lip as I caught the slight gleam of sarcasm in his eyes. "I heard she was still alive. I wanted to see if it was true."

"I suppose Katie told you."

I was silent, wondering if there was anything he did not know about the activities at Balaleigh. "I want to go," I said finally. "I can't stay here forever."

He took my hand, then, conscious of my smart of pain, raised his fingers to my elbow.

"Get back to your room, Maillard," he ordered. "Miss Hannah and I are leaving."

"Not the stairway!" the man called Maillard shouted. "It isn't safe. The master says so."

Richard's voice humored him. "We'll use the safe side. Who is your friend, Maillard?"

"The master," he croaked.

"Was the master always your master?"

"No, sir."

"Who was the master?"

"I was the master."

"Here?"

"In France. Long ago. Long ago."

"Who else is your friend?"

"You, Mr. Richard."

"Who beats you?"

"The mas—" Maillard stopped.

"Does the master give you brew?"

"No, Mr. Richard."

"Who does?"

"You, Mr. Richard."

"Remember that the next time you get out." Richard pressed my elbow gently. "Come, Hannah." He drew me toward the stairs. As we came up to them, I turned and saw Maillard leering at us from the doorway of the room we had left.

"Who is he?" I asked.

Richard did not reply. Instead, he steered me to the right side of the stone stairs. "The safe side," he said. "Follow me and grip the pegs in the wall. Take your time. Don't hurry as you did coming up. You were clambering into the oldest part of the tower as though your life depended upon getting there. For what purpose, Hannah?"

"I've told you, it's you who didn't answer my question."

"Old Maillard is scarcely worth apologizing for when the company is so pleasant. But if you must know—and you're a very persistent young lady, Hannah—he is someone I've known all my life."

"Why is he here?"

"If you knew someone like old Maillard when there's a famine in the country, wouldn't you take him in?"

"Does the master know?"

"Why otherwise? It's the master's house."

"You're being evasive."

"Not really. You're very lovely, you know."

"I'm a peasant girl," I said stubbornly.

"A peasant girl on her way to visit a countess." Again there was that lift of his eyebrows.

I felt my pulses racing. His proximity was distracting. I wanted to be at the bottom of the stairs, to be away from him, to be my own self again, sane, sober and independent. Emotionally, I felt completely at his mercy, ill at ease, unable to cope with his assurance. So I said nothing, treading carefully, hoping that I would not trip. I had no desire to fall against him, to feel once more the rough tweed of his coat against my smarting hands.

Richard walked on silently. But his very silence annoyed me as much as his self-confidence, and to relieve my pent-up emotions, I cried out, "What do I know of anyone here? Who are you, Mr. Richard Ralston? If old Maillard is a mystery to me, so are you. Why are you here at Balaleigh? Why did the master select you to bring me here? What does he want of me? Do you know?"

"I don't, Hannah." Richard's eyebrows shot up again as he turned his head and regarded me with amusement.

"I don't believe you," I said flatly. "You misled me once—why not again?"

"My dear girl, I've never misled you."

"You told me the light I saw in the tower was the moonlight shining through the window. I didn't believe you. I've watched that window night after night, and I knew it wasn't the moon. Now I know old Maillard lives in the tower. I've seen him with my own eyes."

Richard said slowly, "He lives there most of the time, but not always."

"What?"

"Has it occurred to you, Hannah, that a well-brought-up young lady knows when and when not to persist?"

"You're evading the point. I want to know."

"Very well. Old Maillard has a liking for poteen. When he's not up in the hills drinking himself into a stupor verging on insanity, he's up there in the tower. That's when you see the light. When he's away in the hills, there is no light—only the moonlight."

I was silent. He had not mentioned the countess, nor would I. When she returned, there would be time enough for that.

Richard touched my arm. "Why worry about it, Hannah? I'm sorry, I really am. I didn't mean to tantalize you. But above all, my dear, keep away from the tower."

"Why should I?" I asked petulantly.

"There's no devious reason at present why you should or should not except that the master has forbidden it on the grounds of safety."

Walking closely together because of the narrowness of the stairs, we reached a passage leading into the hall. In this way we avoided the great staircase.

"Where do you live when you're not here?" I asked.

A smile lurked at the corners of his mouth. "Where red kangaroos jump on two legs over endless acres and little koalas sleep in the forks of eucalyptus trees and chew the leaves." The caress of his voice was unmistakable.

My curiosity bristled. "What are koalas, pray?"

"Little gray animals with black noses—soft and cuddlesome. They are like a bear, but not a bear." he chucked my chin and drew me against him. "Does that satisfy you, Hannah?" He kissed me lightly on the lips and released me, then walked with long strides down the length of the hall to the front door.

It doesn't, my heart cried out after him. *It doesn't at all.* I wanted to run after him, to bring his head level with mine, to feel the penetration of his eyes and his mouth on mine. But I saw only old Dan bringing in peat to build up the evening fire.

"You'll get the shivers, miss, if I don't keep it burning. I wouldn't like to see you get the shivers."

"Let the fire go out," I said dully.

Unheeding, he went on. "Who cares about the shivers? Not you or the master or Mrs. Rundle. Only old Dan. They force people to eat grass. The grass is hungry like them that don't care. Hungry for death.

Riches they get from grain and pasture, while we die. We die in our thousands, missie. If this fire goes out, one of the blood of Balaleigh dies, too. Will they care then?''

''You're too fanciful,'' I said crossly. I left him and went up to my room. Katie was waiting for me.

''Who is old Maillard?'' I asked when I had settled myself at the dressing table and she had begun to comb my hair. I was throwing discretion to the winds. I did not trust Katie, but nevertheless I knew that if I did not ask her, I would never know.

She regarded me from beneath her eyelashes. In the looking glass I could see that her eyes were furtive. ''I didn't know you knew him, miss.''

I resorted to white-lie strategy. ''I met him coming back from the village.''

''Surely he didn't speak to you.'' Her expression was one of incredulity.

''We passed the time of day. Good gracious, Katie, I must speak to someone.'' Why should I explain myself to the lady's maid? But was she more than the maid? I had begun to wonder. Katie gave the impression that she possessed household privileges beyond her station. I finished lamely, ''He said his name was Maillard.''

''He's a kind of caretaker,'' Katie said, slipping the petticoat over my head. ''He looks after the tower when the old countess is not at Balaleigh. Now that she's coming back for her birthday, he'll have to watch himself. She won't tolerate his drinking poteen the way he does now.''

''When is she coming back?'' I asked.

"In time for her birthday—the sixth of May. It's a great day, miss, or it used to be before things got bad. Lolly buns and balloons and crackers and the old countess swinging there in her chair, especially made in Bath. When they lowered her from the tower on pulleys, she waved her hand and shouted out like a two-year-old. Stand up now, miss, and I'll slip the gown over your head." Katie ran her hand over the gown, smoothing the lace here and there. "My, miss, you're growing prettier every day. And quite plump, too, now that you're getting enough to eat. You'll have to look beautiful tonight, you know, if only for your self-respect."

I looked startled. "Good gracious me! Why?"

Katie smiled coyly. "Didn't you know? Lady Caroline Edly, the earl of Matten's daughter, is coming to dinner. What's more, they say Mr. Richard Ralston fancies her."

CHAPTER SEVEN

Lady Caroline

SEEMINGLY UNAWARE of the tumult she had caused within me, Katie went on dressing me with care. I stared back at myself in the looking glass, knowing instinctively that I would not like Lady Caroline Edly. I had seen her on those rare occasions when hounds and men had met at Balaleigh. Instead of sedately watching from horseback on the Balaleigh common, she was a true member of the meet. Immaculately attired in a black jacket with her sidesaddle habit spread out and attached to the pommel, she was revered but more often jeered at by her fellow huntsmen because of the half brush she wore around her hat.

"She was in at the kill," Katie informed me casually as she slipped a gray poplin gown over my head. "A huntsman handed her the half brush and bloodied her face. Could a man marry a lady like that?" She shivered. "I've heard it told that she didn't like to wipe off the blood, because to be blooded meant she was a true member of the hunt."

My gown boasted lace ruffles at the wrists and a low neckline that offset pearl beads. Katie styled my hair high, and when I viewed myself in the hand mirror, I knew that I looked elegant.

"Lady Caroline is not very pretty," Katie said.

At those words, my spirits rose slightly, and I went down to dinner.

But immediately after I met Lady Caroline, I realized that elegance in itself was no match for vivacity. Lady Caroline was tall in stature, brilliant in conversation and possessed of a self-assurance that commanded respect. She was not, as Katie had said, pretty, although her hair was glossy and her appearance immaculate. Her large hazel eyes looked out confidently from beneath heavy lids. Never for one moment did she expect criticism from others, but rather accepted homage as her own undeniable right.

Richard liked her. His sardonic manner unbent, and his eyes flashed good humor. They complemented each other nicely. Philip and Eton stared open-mouthed at her. The master, however, was glum. Mrs. Scott-Ryan was scantily cordial, and pleading a headache, left the table at the earliest opportunity. Ellen stood behind Lady Caroline's chair, piling food on her plate. I grew despondent and awkward, feeling out of my depth. I did not ride. Hunting jargon was new to me. I sat mesmerized, but knowing that I had nothing to offer, I kept quiet.

I was jealous of the appreciation shining in Richard's eyes. How could I, a peasant girl on sufferance at the Big House, compete with an aristocrat?

I told myself I did not care. She could marry him if that was what she wanted. She could go and live with the red kangaroos and sleepy little gray koalas. She could sail over the seas with Richard Ralston and leave me and my heartbreak alone forever.

I retired as quickly as I could. Contrary to my expectations, I slept heavily and spent the next day in the library, scorning romantic novels and soaking up whatever information I could glean about the Antipodes.

Australia was on the opposite side of the earth from Europe. When it was morning in Ireland, night was closing in over the vast continent called Australia. It was discovered by Captain Cook and, at the command of George III, was settled as a penal colony by Governor Phillip in 1788. It had a Mediterranean climate and exported wool. The meager information and dry facts of the geography books on the library shelves bored me. I could not imagine why Richard had gone to Australia in the first place or why he should want to return. Unless, of course, he hoped to participate in the closely guarded secret of the discovery of gold, which I had heard him mention to the master.

I ate luncheon alone and in the evening pleaded a headache to avoid appearing at dinner, although I surmised that Lady Caroline had gone home after dinner the night before. Later, Katie came quietly into my bedchamber.

I was sitting before the dressing table, gazing at my reflection in the looking glass. Since I had been at Balaleigh, my appearance had improved not only in the quality of the clothes I wore but also in my personal bearing. I felt well. I was more confident. I no longer looked thin. My dark hair was now thick and shining, and my face radiated good health. Pleased with my reflection, I knew that but for the advent of Lady Caroline, Richard would have thought me becoming. A longing seized me to be not only becoming but desirable.

As if my yearning were transparent, Katie came and stood behind me. She picked up a comb and drew it through my hair. "She's just left, miss."

I showed my surprise. "I thought she left yesterday evening after dinner."

"The mist was too thick on the ground for Mr. Richard to drive the gig, and he wanted to show her the stables. She stayed the night. They've been out riding most of the day, and now he's seeing her home."

I did not reply. I hated Katie to guess what I felt about him. The revelation had come so suddenly that I scarcely believed it myself. Her eyes met mine in the looking glass, and I knew it was impossible to hold back anything from her. Every day she dressed me, undressed me and wrapped the bath towel about me when I stepped out of the hipbath. Unobtrusively, she made me aware that she was as familiar with my mind, body and clothes as I was myself.

"Never mind, miss," she said now. "There's more fish in the sea than ever came out of it."

I reared my head haughtily, resenting her sympathy. As I did so, the comb caught a tangle, and my eyes smarted with the teasing irritation.

"Mind what you're doing!" I cried sharply.

Immediately, she put down the comb and, to my consternation, burst into tears. "I'm sorry, miss." She gulped, brushing away the tears with the back of her hand. "I did it for you, miss, honest I did, and now I'm frightened."

"Katie, whatever on earth are you talking about?" I stared at her through the looking glass and saw her wipe her hand on her apron, then plunge it down the front of her gown.

"This, miss." Katie held up a gleaming gold object.

I caught my breath. "What have you there?" I demanded.

"The locket." She dangled it in front of me. "I got it back for you."

"Where did you get it?"

"From the master's bedchamber." She lowered her eyes. "The chambermaid was ill, and I was dusting the room. I saw it there—on the dressing table. Take it, miss. It's yours."

I put my hands behind my back and said, "You had no right to take it."

Katie pouted. "I don't see why. I was only trying to help you, miss."

"Rubbish." Not trusting Katie, I was thoroughly alarmed, dreading the consequences. "You need to remember your station. Leave the room at once. Now. This minute. And take that locket with you. Put it back where you found it."

She grew sulky. "I thought you'd be pleased."

"I am not pleased. I am displeased."

"The locket is yours. You should have it."

"Not until the master returns it himself. Now, go." I pointed to the door.

"Very well, miss. I'm going." She returned the locket to her pocket, and, grimacing slightly, walked to the door. I heard her light footsteps running along the passage. When I was sure that she was gone, I crossed the room and turned the key in the lock, fearing her return with the locket still in her possession.

The delicacy of the situation prevented me from reporting her behavior to the master. Mrs. Scott-Ryan, although she assumed the master's name, had no real authority in the household. The obvious person to approach was Mrs. Rundle. But after her accusation that I had come into possession of the locket through theft, I knew that I would be not only disbelieved but blamed.

I did not look forward to Katie's next appearance in my bedchamber, but much to my relief, I found that I had underestimated her. She appeared each morning and evening when Mary brought the bathwater. Contrary to practice, Mary remained, handing Katie my clothes until I was dressed. Katie was polite, distant and respectful. The locket was not mentioned, nor could it be in front of a third person. Privately, I wondered what she had done with it. The matter dangled silently between us.

Surreptitiously, I began to watch her. One night I saw her creeping down the passage to the master's bedchamber, her gown swathed tightly over her bosom and her fair hair loose about her shoulders. For the first time I became aware of Katie's comeliness. She was of medium height and had a small-boned, well proportioned body; her attractiveness was usually hidden beneath her dark service gown and starched white cap. Instinctively aware of the master's sensuality, I was relieved that I had kept the matter of the locket to myself.

What did I know of any of them—Katie, the master, Mrs. Scott-Ryan and Mrs. Rundle? It seemed they were all saturated with one another, living unto themselves in the small world that was Balaleigh. How did Richard Ralston fit into the pattern? Since the visit of Lady Caroline, I seldom saw him.

I sensed that he was visiting her, and I was determined to put him out of my mind. After all, what did I really know of him? A few stolen kisses had sent my senses spinning. Away from him, I could sustain myself. I was not prepossessing in the worldly sense of Lady Caroline, nor did I have the sensual appeal of Katie. I was merely young and eager for life. Had Richard perceived this latter trait and played upon it with his kisses?

ONE MORNING I started out on my usual walk past the yew forest and toward the hills. I was skirting the old keep when I sensed that Katie was walking behind me. I quickened my pace, instantly aware and dismayed that she also quickened hers. I slowed my footsteps. When she did likewise, I stopped and sat down on one of the boulders, waiting for her to catch up to me.

There were dark shadows beneath her eyes, and her movements were quicker and more intense than usual. She sat down on a boulder opposite me and regarded me gravely.

"I put it back, miss."

"Yes," I said. I did not need to ask her to be more explicit. "I saw you going along to the master's room."

"When?"

"Late one evening."

"What were you doing up that late?"

"I couldn't sleep. I'd gone down to the library to get a book. I was coming back." Once again I found myself justifying my actions to her, but this time, unexpectedly, she burst into tears.

"Mrs. Rundle makes me. I've got to do what Mrs. Rundle says."

"Did she tell you to steal the locket?"

"No, miss, I didn't steal it. I just saw it there. When you didn't want it, I sneaked it back. I'm sorry, miss. I really am. I don't know what came over me."

I decided that magnanimity was the prudent course to take. "Now that it's back, that's all that really matters."

"You mean that, miss?" she asked eagerly.

For the fraction of a second I hesitated. I did not want her for an enemy; neither did I want her as a friend. I recovered quickly. "We have to live together, you know. We can't exist at Balaleigh without coming across each other. Every morning when I wake up, you're there; every night when I go to bed, you're the last person I see."

"It's what I'm here to do, miss."

"If we can't be friendly, it's sensible to call a truce."

"Yes, miss." Her manner was distant but respectful, and I could not avoid seeing tears still in her eyes. "At first, miss, I thought you were ordinary, like the girls at the orphan school. You know, a peasant used to rough ways. It's just since this happened that I've come to know how wrong I was. You're not like that at all. You could almost be a lady."

"I am not a lady," I said. "I was born here at Balaleigh. My mother was a waiting woman who died at my birth. I remained her for seven years. Then, when the master's wife, Lady Berenice, died, I went home to Anna and her husband, my foster parents."

"Yes, miss." I could see that Katie was only politely interested. How I became what I was did not concern her. Her mind was full of herself. She steepled her hands almost in supplication. "I don't want to be sent back to the workhouse. As long as I please Mrs. Rundle and Mrs. Scott-Ryan, there's no fear of that."

"What about Mr. Scott-Ryan?" I asked, curious.

"The master," she gestured helplessly, "he's there to please, too, but beside Mrs. Rundle, he doesn't exactly count."

"But he's the master."

"Mrs. Rundle's got him in the hollow of her hand. She's got everyone in the hollow of her hand."

"Mr. Richard, too?"

Katie shrugged. "He hasn't been here long enough to count."

"Why is he here?" I asked quickly, eager to glean what information I could while Katie was in the mood to give it.

"To marry Lady Caroline, his second cousin. If she had never been born, Mr. Richard would have inherited her father's title and estate. Lord Matten had no other children, you see. The best Mr. Richard could do was to seek his fortune in Australia. Now that he's done that, back he comes to claim his bride.'' Katie looked coy. ''His heart may be elsewhere, but his bread must be buttered and buttered well.''

''You seem to know a great deal about everyone.''

''I was ten when Mrs. Rundle brought me to Balaleigh from the workhouse orphan school. This was after your time here. I've done the rounds at this place ever since. When the orphans are old enough, they are sent out to do domestic service in the big houses. You go from one house to another and back to the workhouse in between rounds. Backward and forward I go from Balaleigh to the workhouse, according to Mrs. Rundle's whims. She's looked after me ever since my mother died. When she couldn't have me with her, she'd send me off to the workhouse. I sort of grew up under its shadow. If I don't please her, off I go; then here I am again, when she's in a fix and needs me.''

I felt sorry for Katie, but she did not gain my sympathy, nor did she expect it. She was too capable and self-sufficient for that. For her, a fact was a fact, something to be coped with in the best way she knew how. And if there was an advantage to be gleaned, none knew better than Katie how to use it.

''What kind of a fix is Mrs. Rundle in now?'' I asked.

Katie regarded me oddly with her head thrown back. ''You're not going to like the answer, miss. She thinks you're living under an assumed name.''

''Good gracious me! What next?''

''You're no more Hannah McCabe than I am.''

"Nonsense. Everyone knows the McCabes are my foster parents."

"That's as may be. Who was your father? Do you know that?"

I stared at her perplexedly.

"You don't know, do you? It's all written on the paper inside the locket."

My eyes narrowed. "Go on."

"If the locket's yours, you must have found the paper yourself."

"The first time I saw that locket was when Anna handed it to me just before I came here." Katie was silent. I grew impatient. "Well, what did the paper say?"

Katie tossed her head. "Why should I tell you?"

"Then why arouse my curiosity?"

"You wouldn't believe me. Just you wait until the master gives the locket back to you—if he ever does." Not waiting for my reply, she rose suddenly from the boulder and ran off along the path that skirted the yew forest.

I sat and watched her go. I thought someone joined her farther on. It looked like Mrs. Rundle, but I was not sure. I got up and walked back toward Balaleigh. As I reached the front garden I saw lady Caroline and Richard Ralston talking at the foot of the stone steps.

"How are you, Hannah?" Lady Caroline's voice was pleasant. "Mr. Ralston was just saying that you don't ride, but I'm sure you wouldn't refuse a drive in the carriage if I called for you tomorrow morning."

I was surprised at her friendliness. "Where are we going?" I asked.

"To Matten House. Mr. Ralston and I thought it might be a nice change for you, my dear."

When I recovered from my surprise and accepted her invitation, she inclined her head graciously, and I felt grateful for the diversion from Katie's deviant disclosures. I was up early the next morning and was already dressed when Katie and Mary appeared to undertake my toilet. Seeing that I donned a warm worsted gown I had not worn before, Katie immediately guessed that I was going out. Not wishing to spoil my anticipated pleasure, I found it easier to tell her where I was bound than to parry her persistent questions. Her face reflected her displeasure, but I ignored it and went down to breakfast.

After I had eaten, I sat outside on a bench facing the front garden awaiting Lady Caroline, who had arranged an early start. When the carriage arrived, I seated myself beside her and was surprised to see Richard riding ahead of us on horseback. As the horses clip-clopped down the driveway, I glanced back at Balaleigh and saw Katie looking out from an upstairs window. But the weather was fine, and I had no intention of allowing my maid to mar my day.

I had thought of Lady Caroline only as a huntswoman and a possible wife for Richard Ralston. Now I realized that she was also a philanthropist who used much of the large fortune she had inherited from her mother to relieve the famine-stricken tenant farmers of much of their plight.

"You see devastation everywhere," she said, deftly managing the horses with her gloved hands. "Farmhouses and villages are deserted, walls and hedges are in decay, and abandoned fields are invaded by rushes, bracken and scrub. It's heartbreaking when you think how pleasant everything used to be.''

I felt I had no answer to the obvious, and we drove along in companionable silence. I knew we were following the road that led to the place of the McCabe eviction. I gripped my thumbs between my fingers in an attempt to brace myself for the inevitable.

"Do you hunt?" Lady Caroline asked.

"No."

"Drive?"

"No."

"What do you do?"

"I used to assist at the hedge schools."

"Really!"

"You sound surprised."

"Only because you're so young." She laughed lightly. "I find it hard to reconcile you with some of those village bumpkins."

"My foster father was also a teacher. It made things easier for me."

"I thought he was a peasant."

"He was a priest who fled to the continent after supporting the Relief Bill that would admit native Irish into the British Parliament. When he returned, he was defrocked because he married my foster mother. He grew potatoes on the allotment. After he died of famine fever, we were evicted."

Lady Caroline put the reins in one hand and patted my knee, and I sensed that Richard had acquainted her with what he knew about my presence at Balaleigh. "The name Hannah has a Biblical sound, has it not?"

"Indeed, yes. But it's also an Irish rural name. You hear it in these parts."

"And McCabe?"

"Gallowglasses—mercenary soldiers who came from the Western Isles about 1350 'to conquer or to die' in the service of an Irish earl. I take my name from my foster parents."

She regarded me thoughtfully. "My forebears received their lands from King Edward the Third in the fourteenth century to uphold royal power against the native Irish. The title came later. They may have thrown bows and arrows at your adventurous gallowglasses and the Irish earl from the other side of the hedgerows—who knows?" Her voice was light, neither patronizing nor condescending, and I wondered why she was making the effort to be so gracious.

Richard joined us. "The cabins are gone, Hannah."

I felt miserable. It was difficult to distinguish this part of the winding road without the landmark of the cabins on their half-acre allotments. I wondered what had happened to Rose Mullarkey and her son, Billy, whom Anna had thought I might marry one day. I wondered, too, about Anna and the little girls. But I curbed my sentiment and merely asked, "Evictions?"

He nodded grimly. "On the Balaleigh estate, cabins give way to grazing land or grain fields."

After some time we reached Matten House. To my amazement, a large number of ragged peasants were lined up outside the main entrance. The lodge keeper opened the huge iron gates to admit us and touched his forelock as we passed through. The peasants made no attempt to press forward. They stood waiting patiently, almost resignedly.

"This is what I've brought you to see," Lady Caroline said. "I want you both to be aware of what we're doing here for our tenants. Instead of evicting them and turning their allotments into grazing land, we're giving them all the help we can."

Flattered that I should be included in plans that were of momentous importance to her, I asked, "What kind of help?"

"We've set up a famine-relief kitchen. When the agent is satisfied that families can't pay their rent, they are admitted here for a meal once a day. I'm sure you'd like to see it in operation."

Conscious that she had left me no option, I was, nevertheless, as anxious as Richard to see the relief system working.

At twelve o'clock a gong sounded and the iron gates were opened. In orderly files, the peasants walked up the driveway to a kitchen set up in a rotunda not far from the gates. Once the peasants were admitted, they received an individual ration of bread and drippings and a bowl of soup. Sitting at trestle tables, they ate their meal, after which those who needed clothes proceeded to the exchange, where they received more suitable garments.

"We burn the rags," Lady Caroline explained. "Disease can take its toll."

The estate steward to whom Lady Caroline introduced us was eager for Richard's opinion on the extension of the soup kitchen. I sat alone with Lady Caroline, wondering why he had solicited Richard's viewpoint; I assumed that Richard was as ignorant of such matters as I was myself. But Lady Caroline answered my unspoken thoughts.

"You may not know it, Hannah, but Richard is active in relief work and organizing food distribution in Ireland. He's also involved with plans to encourage emigration to Australia. Shepherds, shearers and laborers are needed to work the huge sheep stations and wheat farms. Their decision to emigrate also relieves the distress here."

So that was where Richard went on his absences from Balaleigh. I watched him and the steward talking earnestly for some time; then Richard joined us, obviously in a satisfied frame of mind.

We spent a worthwhile day with Lady Caroline that was not devoid of pleasantness. We did not go to the house for lunch. Instead, we ate it in the rotunda kitchen, partaking of the same fare as the tenants but waited on by servants. After Lady Caroline had taken us to view the huge parkland and grain fields, we had small cakes and wine in the drawing room of Matten House. Richard promised to draw the master's attention to the care of peasants on the Matten estate. Then Lady Caroline drove me back in the carriage, and Richard rode beside us.

"What a wonderful day!" I exclaimed to him after we had bidden Lady Caroline farewell at the threshold of Balaleigh.

He did not commit himself, nor had I expected him to. He merely gave me his familiar quizzical raising of the eyebrows and remarked, "You must learn to ride, Hannah. There's a quiet gray in the stables that will be just the horse for you."

CHAPER EIGHT

The Riding Habit

THE LOCKET was on my mind all the time. I knew nothing of what it might contain, if anything. I wondered if Katie had been bluffing or if she really did know something about its contents. If so, she would, of course, tell Mrs. Rundle. Of that I was certain. The fear of returning to the workhouse hung like a constant cloud over her head, and Mrs. Rundle's favor was the necessary component of its removal.

I did not know who my father was. No one, least of all Anna McCabe, had ever mentioned him to me. I had assumed that because my mother was a serving woman, my father was also of lowly station, a groom, perhaps, or a stablehand, who had pleasurably pursued my mother and made her pregnant in an offhand kind of way.

But conjecture was of no avail, and I decided to bide my time. When the locket was returned to me—if ever it was—I would then have the opportunity to make myself as wise as Katie purported to be.

"Can you read?" I asked her one night as she prepared me for retiring.

She looked at me warily. "Of course, miss."

"And write?"

"Yes."

"Where did you learn?"

"In the workhouse orphan school."

I was silent. She was possibly telling the truth. I knew little about the orphan schools attached to the workhouses.

Presently, after she had slipped my nightgown over my head, she said, "You think I don't know enough to read the name I saw on the paper inside the locket. Well, I do." She finished my toilet quickly, dropped me a mock curtsy and marched out of the room with her head held high.

The master was away for the next few days, and Richard took the responsibility of asking Tom, the groom, to teach me to ride on Dolly, the gray mare.

I did not have a riding habit, but Katie, always on the alert, suggested I use an old one in the attic. "I'll rummage it out for you," she said. "It's just the thing you want."

Surprised that she should be so enthusiastic about my new venture, I accepted the habit when she brought it to me. The costume of dark blue serge was in good condition and fit me very well. Katie bundled my hair into a bun at the back of my neck, and when she put the hat on me, the person looking back at me through the mirror appeared a stranger.

Katie giggled, whether with delight at the transformation or nervousness at the change she had wrought, I was not sure. "You look the part, miss, and soon your riding will match it."

Richard, in riding attire, met me at the side door, and we walked together along the path leading to the stables. They were warm, well ventilated and free from drafts. I could smell fresh hay in the hayloft over the stalls. Dolly was already saddled and waiting on the pavement of hard Dutch bricks. As she had not yet been exercised, Tom put her through the paces to which she had been trained. Afterward, he helped me mount then walked beside me and steadied Dolly with the reins as I led her around the enclosure.

"Well done," he said when the lesson was finished. "She's a quiet horse, easy to manage. In a short time you'll be trotting, cantering and galloping her."

So absorbed had I been with the lesson that I did not notice that Richard had ridden off along the road to a far field. Feeling stiff, I went back to the house and up to my room, where Katie, smirking, took off my habit.

The riding lessons became the usual routine of the next two mornings. I felt I was progressing very well and looked forward to the time when I could take Dolly out on my own.

I was coming down the staircase the following day in my riding habit when I saw the master at the bottom of the stairs, staring upward. His face was white, and he held himself stiffly. I bade him good morning and stood waiting, as he appeared to be on the point of addressing me.

"Don't you good morning me!" he cried, ready to explode with rage. "What is the meaning of this—this masquerade?"

Unsure of myself, I managed to say, "I'm on my way to the riding lesson."

"Don't speak in riddles, miss! What riding lesson?"

"The lessons Mr. Richard arranged for me when you were away."

"Egad! He did, did he? Where did you get that costume?"

"It was in the attic."

"Who gave you permission to ransack the attic?"

I stared at him, too scared to reply.

"Mrs. Rundle!" he bellowed. "Mrs. Rundle!"

She approached with miraculous rapidity. Behind her, advancing with less speed, was Mrs. Scott-Ryan. Neither woman looked over my head this time. Both faced me squarely.

Mrs. Rundle snorted. "What did I tell you?"

"It's too much. Too much," Mrs. Scott-Ryan wailed. "Why should I be subjected to this? Tell her to take it off, Scott-Ryan. Please!"

"She can do that in her bedchamber." Mrs. Rundle gave me a push up the stairs and turned to the master. "It's what I said, sir. It's been like this every morning, with her coming down in that habit as though she were her ladyship herself. My! How she came by it, I don't know."

"She claims to have found it in the attic, Mrs. Rundle."

"In that case, she's not to be trusted. If she ransacks the attic, what next?"

I turned around and faced them. "What I have done, I've done in all good faith. Mr. Richard will bear that out."

"Don't hide behind Mr. Richard," Mrs. Rundle sneered.

"Mr. Richard is away," the master added.

"Take me upstairs," Mrs. Scott-Ryan moaned. "I need to sal volatile."

"When will Mr. Richard be back?" I asked the master.

Before he could reply, Mrs. Rundle snapped, "Don't stand there and ask your impudent questions. Move aside and allow Mrs. Scott-Ryan to pass."

I did so. As Mrs. Scott-Ryan mounted the stairs, I saw that she was sobbing uncontrollably into her handkerchief. I was wondering what had upset her to such an extent when the master's voice boomed out, "Upstairs to your room, miss, and take off that—that attire. Give it to Katie to put in the attic."

Inwardly quaking at my apparent misdemeanor, I expected him to order me to the library for the express purpose of chiding me for my willful ways. But he merely turned his back and strode down the hall to the open front door.

Mrs. Rundle followed Mrs. Scott-Ryan upstairs. I waited until they had disappeared before I retreated to my bedchamber. As I expected, Katie had preceded me. Without a word, I forestalled her by taking off the riding habit and handing it to her. She appeared nonplussed.

"Take it," I said. "The master wishes you to put it in the attic."

To my amazement, she burst into tears. "It's my fault, miss. I should have left it where it was!"

"Whose habit is it?"

"Don't you know, miss? I thought you did. It belonged to Lady Berenice. Mrs. Rundle said you looked like two peas in a pod. The master saw it, too. That's what made him so angry. It's all there in the locket, miss, if only you could get it back. We say in the kitchen there's a look about you like the lady on the stairs."

"The lady on the stairs," I repeated dully. I wanted to stop Katie's flow of eloquence. I resented hearing intimate disclosures from the maid who washed me, dressed me, smirked at me. Yet if I stopped her fluency, who else was there to acquaint me with what she knew?

"Lady Berenice, miss, the master's wife who died. When he saw you coming down the stairs in her riding habit, he thought he'd seen a ghost, and it was only morning, and the fire was hot, and the sunshine was coming in through the hall door. It wasn't the time for ghosts, was it, miss? Yet there you were, so like her."

My face set in a hard line. I refused to be swept along into an admission of which I had no proof. "You're talking nonsense," I said.

"If Lady Berenice had lived, she would have been the next countess when the old countess dies. Now there's no one else—only her, a toothless old hag who should have died long ago, and Mr. Scott-Ryan. He can't succeed, nor can Mr. Philip or Mr. Eton or other pretenders. Balaleigh is no place for illegitimates, or pretenders, as they call the young men in the kitchen. But as long as the old countess lives, the master is lord of the manor."

"What happens when she dies? Did the gossips inform you of that?"

Katie had the grace to hang her head. Her voice was hoarse as she whispered, "We could all of us become famine victims—the master, Mrs. Scott-Ryan, you, everyone—because the house has no heirs and goes to the crown. The Court of Chancery, they call it in Great Britain, and whether we like it or not, we are ruled by it."

After Katie had gone up to the attic with the riding habit, I donned my gray gingham gown and went downstairs. As I passed the portrait of Lady Berenice, I kept my eyes fixed rigidly ahead. When the opportune moment came, I would look long and hard at the lady purported to be my mother. But, conscious of prying eyes, I resolved to refuse them the satisfaction of seeing that my curiosity was aroused.

Nevertheless, my thoughts were full of Katie's disclosures, and I found myself delving back into my childhood, trying to piece together possible proof.

In this frame of mind, I went out the side door and made my way to the stables. Dolly was nowhere to be seen, nor were Tom or Mr. Bede, the coachman. Pete, the stableboy, was sweeping the brick pavement in front of the stalls.

"You're too late, miss," he said. "Dolly's gone out for exercise. She's not had her proper run since you've been riding her."

Red-faced, I turned away. Then, to my surprise and delight, I saw Richard riding across the far field toward me.

"No riding lesson?" he asked when he had dismounted beside me.

I shook my head.

"Why not?"

I told him, conscious of the triviality of the incident and leaving out Katie's explanation.

"I entirely overlooked the fact that I should have told him," Richard said.

"How could you? The master was away when I began my riding lessons."

"Where is the gray now?"

"The groom's taken her out for exercise."

"Egad! That's unfortunate. I'll make it my business to acquaint the master of the oversight at the first opportunity."

With Richard leading his horse, we walked back to the house. My heart had ceased to thump and my blood to race. It seemed the most natural thing in the world that Richard should walk beside me, and I felt unexpectedly happy. I tried not to think of Lady Caroline and my own shortcomings. Richard did not kiss me as he had done on previous occasions, nor did I wish him to. I did not doubt for one moment that he could still set my pulses racing and my senses lurching. But now the sun shone on the green hills, bright with broom, furze and rhododendrons, and I felt warm and contented. I was enjoying Richard's company in a way I had not thought possible.

In the afternoon I went to the library. It was empty, as it usually was at this time of day. I ran my eye along the shelves, passing over the thick leather-bound volumes until I came to a small pamphlet wedged in between two books on the History of Europe. I took it down from the shelf, brushing the dust from its upper section with my handkerchief. Obviously it had not been used for some time. I sat down near the door and opened the pamphlet. Anyone entering the room would see me immediately, and in this way, I reasoned, I could not be accused of eavesdropping. But no one came in, and I had the library to myself.

I read intently, occasionally jotting down facts to clarify my comprehension. The date on the flyleaf, written in finely formed figures, was 1832, two years after I was born. As the afternoon progressed, the room grew darker; and when a fine rain began to fall, I could no longer see to read. No one had come in to turn on the oil lamps or light the fire. I put the pamphlet back on the shelf and went upstairs to dress for dinner.

When I entered the bedchamber, Katie and Mary were whispering together in a corner. Mary scuttled away, leaving Katie and me alone. While I recognized her efficiency, I longed for moments of privacy in my room. Her contradictions—saying one thing and meaning another, pretending to be my friend when in reality she was not—bewildered me. I had too much common sense to expect or even want her friendship, but the fact that she offered it amazed me. Peasant born but well educated, and now in a different station of life at Balaleigh, I knew as well as Katie what was expected of a lady's maid. And that was most certainly not friendship.

Her untruths had led me to distrust her, and so I had become wary of her without really liking her. As we were constantly in each other's company—I could not escape her morning or night—I tried to excuse her actions on the grounds that she was frightened of Mrs. Rundle, whose masterful attitude was indeed frightening.

I wished I were composed enough in the master's presence to say, "Please free me from my lady's maid. I've dressed myself, washed myself and combed my hair all my life. I want to continue to do these things for myself. I don't want a maid constantly at my elbow." But even if I were brave enough, I knew the request would be to no avail. It was not only the master with whom I must contend. It was also Mrs. Rundle, and behind Mrs. Rundle I could see the pungent face of Katie peering at me as even now she was peering at me in the looking glass.

"Miss, the locket's gone."

I did not reply.

She raised her voice. "It's gone, miss. I can't find it anywhere."

"What in the name of fortune are you talking about, Katie?" As I said this, I knew she must see through my subterfuge. She was intelligent, but I was not going to admit that the locket was on my mind, even more so now than previously.

"You know, miss. You know very well."

I considered. "How do you know it's gone?"

"The master's moved it. It used to be on his dressing table. Now it's not there anymore."

"You seem to know a great deal about the master's bedchamber."

She did not avert her eyes as she had done on another occasion when she had mentioned details of the master's room. "It's as I said, miss. I go there because—Mrs. Rundle sends me. She—she's had a difference with the master."

I felt suddenly sorry for Katie. So young, so worldly-wise, yet caught up in the lust of the master, the possessiveness of Mrs. Rundle and the passivity of Mrs. Scott-Ryan.

"I put the riding habit back in the attic, miss. Don't wear it any more. Better to be as you are than a pretender like those other two—Philip and Eton. When the old countess dies, there will be no one to inherit."

"She may not die for a long time," I said.

"The toothless old hag—she should have been dead long ago."

"Why do you say that?"

"It's all to the master's interests to keep her alive. I've told you, miss. Without her, he'd have to go." Our eyes met in the looking glass. "What's out there for any of us? A famine grave, hungry grass and the wailing of the banshee. We'll know soon enough when she dies—the fire in the hall will go out. Not all Dan's peat will keep it alive. A dead fire in a dead house and the wind wailing and the ghosts rattling the doors and windows and the lost souls shrieking until our ears are deaf from the sound. Who cares, who cares, *who cares,* I ask?"

"Katie, don't!" I cried, alarmed at her loss of control.

"All may be well. I—I want you to know that you can't rely on me—you've probably found that out—

but if I possibly can, I'll do the best for you. The best I can." Beating her breasts, she walked to the door. Her body shook with convulsive movements, back and forth. The sound of keening grew louder. "The workhouse for all of us," she sobbed, hammering her hands on the door. "Not the assizes, prison or transportation but the workhouse. Did you hear, miss?"

"Katie!"

But she did not heed me. She pulled at the door and went out and only the breeze through the opening gave evidence that she had been in the room.

CHAPTER NINE

The Wonder of the Age

I HAD BEEN LUCKY to find the pamphlet. It was the only way I could glean any information. The wall of silence surrounding the countess was no longer absolute. At least I could read about her. Now that the locket was beyond my reach, I had miraculously found another source.

I breakfasted early and made my way to the library. The pamphlet was where I had left it, wedged in tightly between two heavy tomes outlining the History of Europe. It was entitled *The Wonder of the Age*; or *The Story of the Countess of Balaleigh*. I reread the preface, then went on to the main events in the countess's life.

Born in 1745, the year of the final defeat of the Jacobites, the countess had known most of the crowned heads of Europe. At the same time, as a countess in her own right, she consolidated the Balaleigh estate by entering the grain market and converting the holdings into pasture land.

Married to an untitled English gentleman with a seat in the Commons at Westminster, she had a daughter,

Lady May, and a granddaughter, Lady Berenice; both women stood in the line of succession. It was whispered that the fairies had caused the disappearance of the male line, preferring to see the female sex preserving and multiplying the fairy rings that sprang up everywhere on the Balaleigh estate.

With the death of Lady May after a miscarriage, Lady Berenice, now heiress to the title and estate, was brought up under the domination of the countess. At eighteen, Lady Berenice gave birth to a child. Shortly afterward, she went to France, sent there, it was rumored, by an irate and humiliated countess in an endeavor to cover up her granddaughter's misdemeanor. Two years later, Lady Berenice returned to marry Philip Scott-Ryan, who, at her premature death, became master of Balaleigh.

No mention was made of the illegitimate child. As far as the family was concerned, it might never have been.

Old, decrepit and approaching senility, the countess still reigned in her own right. As long as she lived, Scott-Ryan would continue to run the estate, but on her death and in the absence of heirs, Balaleigh would pass to the lord chancellor's court.

Small wonder, I thought, that the master promoted the countess far and wide when she was away from Balaleigh and heralded her return. The pamphlet described her as the wonder of the age. Now, at one-hundred-and-three years old, I knew she had a more practical role to fill. She was the rock to which all at Balaleigh clung. She was more than an eccentric old woman. In the absence of heirs, she epitomized security.

Could I prove that Lady Berenice was my mother? After the episode of the riding habit, I was neither stunned nor surprised by the revelation. Indeed, it seemed as though I had always known. The knowledge was part of me. But if I proved that I were indeed her illegitimate daughter, I would have no rights. I would stand where Philip and Eton, the master's illegitimate sons, already stood.

I shut the pamphlet and put it back on the shelf. Then I went out into the hall and stared up at the portrait of the countess. Thus it was that I received a shock that sent shivers down my spine. I could scarcely believe my eyes. It was incredible that I had not noticed it before. Hanging around the countess's neck, blending in with the multicolored threads of her brocade gown so as to be scarcely visible, was the golden locket that, since my arrival, had caused so much consternation in the household. It was the locket that Anna McCabe had thrust into my hand.

"The paper is in the locket," Katie had said. I could believe now that the ornamental gold case contained answers to my queries. But, apart from this, the vital issue remained, hammering at my brain with insistent uncertainty. Why was I here? What purpose was I serving at Balaleigh?

I had no one to ask, no one to confide in. I was alone. Richard might cause my senses to pulsate, but beyond that, he was out of reach.

What was my future? I felt despondent, low in spirit, and wondered how I would fill my days.

I went down to the side door and walked toward the front garden. Water was running smoothly in the fountain; fuchsias and bluebells were growing beside the water; a wren was hopping in and out of a nearby hedge. I had thought to be quiet for a while, but coming down the slope toward the fountain, I saw the master and Richard. Both were absorbed in conversation.

"I did not forbid her to ride the horse," I heard the master say, "I objected to her wearing the habit of my late wife." He raised his voice as he caught sight of me. "Miss!"

"Yes, sir." I dropped a small curtsy to both men.

His eagle eyes passed over my body and rested on my face. "Did you return that habit to the attic?"

"I asked my maid to do so."

"Who is your maid?"

"Katie."

"I should have thought Katie has enough to do without being further encumbered."

"I was merely complying with your wishes, sir. It was you who detailed that Katie should take it to the attic." Although my heart had leaped at the suggestion that Katie's duties might be curtailed, he did not pursue the point.

"Are you satisfied?" he asked Richard.

"Perfectly, sir."

I was about to proceed along the path when Richard said softly, "May I have your attention for a moment, Hannah?"

"Of course." I stopped, but he caught my arm and drew me toward the yew forest. The master stared after us, then turned on his heel and headed for the house.

Richard opened the iron gate that led into the forest. "Have you been in here before, Hannah?"

I shook my head. The yew trees were planted so closely together that a perpetual gloom reigned overhead.

"It's called the Countess's Retreat," Richard explained as we walked on. "In her heyday she used to come here to think over the many problems that beset her." He grimaced. "She's an obstinate old lady, and most of the problems have been of her own making."

"Have you seen her?"

"Only when she's lowered from the west tower in her Bath chair on high days and holidays. Have you?"

"No. When I lived here as a little girl, she didn't do that sort of thing. In fact—" I paused ruminatively "—I don't remember ever seeing her, although everyone was very afraid of her. I think she must have gone away for long periods."

"She still does. She spends the winter in Dublin, the summer in Amboise. She comes home for her birthday."

I made no response, and he headed for the path that wound among the trees to a small summerhouse fitted with rustic wooden benches. We sat down.

"What a beautiful place," I said with delight, looking around.

He squeezed my hand. "A beautiful place for a beautiful lady. You are beautiful, you know, with the wind lifting your dark hair and bringing up the color in your cheeks. May I kiss you, Hannah?"

I smiled. "You've never asked permission before. You've just kissed me."

"Is that so?"

I felt his arm about my waist. He drew me against him. Lightly, his lips touched mine.

"Hannah."

"Yes?"

"Kiss me."

"I—think we've kissed enough." I pushed him away. "You—you forget. There's Lady Caroline."

"What!"

"Do you bring her here and kiss her as you do me?" I felt my jealousy rising, but I could not control it.

"Why ever on earth should I want to kiss Lady Caroline?"

"I thought you were interested in her."

"Hannah, is this a figment of your imagination?" Almost roughly, he pressed my body against his. "Do you think I would act like this if I were wooing another woman?" His lips brushed against mine, and suddenly I could not breathe. His mouth moved away from mine and planted a trail of kisses down my neck. I began to struggle.

"Leave me alone. Please—please."

He straightened himself and stood up. "On an occasion like this, Hannah, a man does not apologize. He merely hopes that at another time he may be more favorably received." When I did not answer, he shrugged nonchalantly, and turning away from me, strode slowly off down the path. I was alone in the yew forest.

The shadows lengthened, and the air grew cold. I needed to collect my pent-up emotions. In a moment, when I knew I could not possibly catch up with Richard, I would make my way to the house. But I had not counted on company. To my dismay, I saw the master walking toward me. He gave me a swift glance, taking in my flushed face and ragged breathing.

"So you're not to be trusted," he observed. "Where is Mr. Ralston?"

"I—I don't know," I mumbled, feeling like a child caught in a guilty act.

He clicked his tongue against his cheek. "I'm not blind, girl, or countenancing. If you choose to behave like this, the best place for you is the workhouse." He came close to me, and I could smell the whiskey on his breath. "Unless...you share your favors." His coarse hand tore at the bodice of my gown. I felt the cool air on my naked skin as his lips came down on my flesh.

"Get away!" I cried. "Get away!"

Breathing heavily, he groped at my bosom, while I tried to twist away from him. He was a heavy man, and I doubted his agility. I ceased to struggle. He mistook my inertness for willingness, and in a brief cessation of his overtures, I managed to push him forcibly from me. He staggered, overshot his balance and fell to the ground.

I ran down the path to the iron gate and along the pavement to the side door of the house. Mercifully, no one was about. I skimmed up the stairs and, panting, reached my bedchamber. It was empty. Katie was not there. Breathless, I sank down onto my bed.

Katie did not appear to dress me for dinner, and I assumed that the master had made other arrangements for her. I changed into my dinner gown of blue silk with ruffles at the neck and sleeves, relieved that my inner commotion had subsided. I picked up the gown I had just discarded and considered ways of mending the torn bodice. Finding it beyond repair, I put the gown in the corner of the wardrobe.

After the gong had sounded, I went slowly downstairs, wondering how I could face up to a situation with both Richard and the master present. I need not have worried. They did not appear. Both had been invited to dine with Lady Caroline at Matten.

During the next few days, when I did meet them individually face-to-face, each was careless in his approach to me and had seemingly forgotten the incident. But I could not fail to notice the gravel rash on the master's hands and new that I could never brace myself to ask the vital questions nagging at me. I could not go to him and demand the return of the locket and the reason for my being here. I was dependent on his pleasure.

Although Katie did not now attend me in the evenings or wait upon my toilet in the mornings, she continued to look after my room and my clothes. I was therefore not surprised when I came into my room one morning after breakfast to find her sitting at the window, mending my bodice.

"What happened to it, miss?" she asked.

"An accident," I said. "In the yew forest."

"Did you slip?"

"I tore it on an overhanging bough." I felt my face flushing and knew she did not believe me, but she accepted the explanation with a grimace and went on with the mending. I waited for her to make some reference to the cessation of her duties as my maid, but she did not. Likewise, I also decided to ignore it.

"I don't think I can do much with this," she said, holding up the bodice.

"Give the gown to Mary, or better still, put it in the furnace."

"Not under Mrs. Rundle's prying eyes. If you go away from here, you might be able to wear a scarf to hide the patch."

"I'm not going away," I said, wondering what she was talking about.

Katie did not reply, merely folded the gown and put it away in the wardrobe.

Each day I continued to go into the library. On a small side table was a brown, rectangular, polished calendar box showing the days and months of the year. The pages had not been turned in a long time. Now I made it my business to twist the wooden knob so that all who entered the library might know the correct date. Today was April 6.

The disclosures of the pamphlet were much on my mind, and I read and reread it in an endeavor to glean what I could from between the lines. This afternoon, as I opened it, I saw written in ink on the flyleaf, "Suppressed before distribution." I looked at it hard, sure that these words had not been there yesterday. When I considered the contents, particularly those concerning Lady Berenice, it did not surprise me that the information had been suppressed. I was trying to remember if I had seen the inscription before when Mrs. Rundle marched into the library and bore down upon me forcefully.

"What have you there, may I ask?"

I shut the pamphlet. "It's no business of yours, Mrs. Rundle."

"That's as may be. You've been nothing but a constant source of trouble ever since you've come here. Put that book back, miss, where you got it from."

I got up and sauntered to the shelves, away from the volumes on the History of Europe and toward the encyclopedias. I placed the pamphlet between two volumes about plants of the world. I knew where to find it, but so also did Mrs. Rundle.

The master entered the library. He nodded briefly at Mrs. Rundle, ignored me and began to rummage in the desk drawer.

"What is the date of today?" he boomed at Mrs. Rundle.

"The sixth of April." Mrs. Rundle flicked her eyes to the calendar box as though she were responsible for keeping it current. "Surely a date to remember."

I wondered what was special about this particular day and saw a meaningful look pass between Mrs. Rundle and the master.

Then, suddenly, came the sound of bells. All the bells of the house seemed to be ringing at once, echoing and reechoing throughout the rooms. Outside, the gloom of late afternoon was suddenly brightened by a blaze of lights from the west tower.

"Egad!" The master strode to the window. "The countess has come home!"

CHAPTER TEN

The Return of the Countess

THE MASTER and Mrs. Rundle hastened from the library. I did not follow, nor was I expected to do so. I sat in the library, watching the tower, wondering how an old lady of 103 years had mounted the crumbling stairs. I conjured up visions of old Dan and old Maillard carrying her up the stairs in a huge chair. Unless—and I gasped with surprise—there was another, easier way of ascent.

As Katie dressed me for dinner, I sensed her excitement, but she refrained from making more than a few comments and hurried away as soon as possible.

Would the countess be present for dinner? But when the gong sounded and I entered the dining room, the master and Mrs. Scott-Ryan sat stolidly in their seats. Philip and Eton, still at home before returning to Cambridge on April 24 for the Easter term, failed to contribute their usual titters to the meal. And so we ate in silence, with Ellen waiting on table.

I wondered what difference the return of the countess would make. Would she conquer the stairs and sweep through the house, demanding that we all spring to our feet and imposing new duties upon us? Would she assert herself to such an extent that we would regard her with awe? But she was not Mrs. Rundle or Mrs. Scott-Ryan. She was the countess of Balaleigh, an old lady who had returned home, not to ordain but to look forward to her one hundred and third birthday.

Nothing untoward happened. Save for the brightly lit tower each evening, we never saw her. Life at Balaleigh went on much the same as before, removed from the outside world.

Mrs. Rundle carried out her duties sullenly, seldom addressing the master and taking things very much into her own hands. She might have been the countess herself, so much did the servants, with the exception of Katie, stand in awe of her. Katie, I now learned, despite her so-called fear of the housekeeper, heeded her to a minimal degree and then only when it coincided with her own interests.

Mrs. Scott-Ryan retired more often than not to her room, appearing briefly and wordlessly at dinner, a mere shadow of her former self. Ignored by the master and Mrs. Rundle, ridiculed by Philip and Eton and patronized by Katie and Mary, she moped about the house in a long blue satin dressing gown that was a relic of more splendid days. Philip and Eton continued to titter, giggle and nudge, about what I was never quite sure.

At the first available opportunity, when I was certain that my movements were not observed, I went to the library and retrieved the pamphlet. Fearful that Mrs. Rundle, who had watched me put it on the shelf, might remove and confiscate it, I hesitated, wondering where to hide it. If I put it back in its first position between the two volumes on European history, whoever had written the suppression date on the fly-leaf might return and take the pamphlet away.

I found a new hiding place. A book entitled *The History of European Art* was covered with a dark, homemade book cover. It was easy to insert the pamphlet into the lining on the back of the front cover. I returned the book to the shelf, satisfied that the pamphlet would not be found easily.

Much to my surprise, Richard began to solicit my company. Or at least I thought he was. He often came into the library when I was reading and engaged me in conversation. One afternoon, on returning from a walk in the hills, I met him also returning from some undisclosed destination. At first I thought he might have been visiting Lady Caroline, but he was walking, not riding. I dismissed my surmise as none of my business and was happy when he not only joined me but held my hand as we walked over the green grass and yellow furze.

"If I can't kiss you," he said with a sidelong glance, "I can at least get to know you."

I longed for him to take me in his arms and kiss me as he had done in the yew forest, but I remained silent, knowing that I dared not trust myself to speak.

"It doesn't suit you, Hannah," he remarked after some time.

"What doesn't?"

"This—this pushing aside what is good for us both."

I stopped walking. "Kissing has gone out of fashion," I said rather primly.

"Not with the furze about. It only flowers once, you know." With a deft movement, he put his arm around my waist. "I could devour you," he said, his eyes on my mouth.

"Please don't." Suddenly flustered, I pushed him away.

"Do you love me, Hannah?"

"I don't—know."

"We could be happy together, you and I. As it is—" He hesitated, then went on firmly. "There's a kind of family arrangement—for me to marry Lady Caroline."

My hand continued to rest in his. "What else?"

"Absolutely nothing. I came over her to claim my bride, but Lady Caroline has no intention of going to Australia with me. She's immersed in good works—workhouse reform and that sort of thing."

"Are you in love with her?"

"No." His voice was emphatic.

I did not probe, and he told me no more. Slowly and silently, we walked back along the road to Balaleigh.

Soon afterward I discovered that he went riding daily with Lady Caroline. I was not jealous, merely stunned. I wished that he had not attempted amorous advances with me or even told me of his feelings for Lady Caroline. It would have been easier to accept the fact as it was. I knew now that I was in love with Richard, totally and irrevocably.

I tried to hide it. I confided in no one, but despite my reticence, Katie seemed to know. She did not allude to it; rather, she spoke in riddles.

"The old countess is watching you, miss. There's nothing she doesn't see from her window."

"Don't be absurd. Why should she watch me?"

Katie idled with a hairbrush. "She may be more interested in you than you think."

"Fiddlesticks."

"Have you found your locket?" she asked carelessly.

"No."

"Every time I go into the master's room, I look for it, but it's never there."

"Perhaps you should forget it."

"Then why do you go on prying, trying to find out things?"

"Katie, what are you talking about?"

"That pamphlet. Mrs. Rundle told me to destroy it, the one she found you reading."

"Why?"

Katie shrugged. "Perhaps she thinks you might overstep the mark—get ideas about yourself, you know—and the countess can't last forever."

I chose to ignore her veiled curiosity. "Did you destroy it?"

"No. I couldn't find it."

I was both glad and relieved; glad that the evidence was still there and relieved that I had hidden the pamphlet successfully.

My passion for Richard took a more even course. Away from him, I found my daily life easier. Without consummation, our love affair was edgy, and I wondered if he would indeed marry Lady Caroline.

The sudden announcement of their betrothal put my doubts at rest. Richard scarcely seemed to hear me when I offered my congratulations. Lady Caroline, momentarily forgetful of good works, was effervescent with excitement. I felt sorry for them both, then sorrier still for myself. Without Richard I was lost. There was no one else on my horizon. But Richard had aroused my bodily desires, and I dreaded the day when I must take a husband less in caliber than he.

A day later, Katie took me into her confidence, swearing me to secrecy. "The master's going to marry me, miss."

"You don't love him, or do you?"

"That groping old man? No, miss, of course not."

"Is it worth it?"

"It will make me mistress of Balaleigh. Anything is worth that."

"Not for long. The old countess might die soon. What then?"

"Nothing Mrs. Rundle can't manage. She arranged this, and she'll see that I get my dues—as long as I don't run afoul of her."

"What about Mrs. Scott-Ryan?"

"She lost the master years ago. You wondered where all those elegant gowns in your wardrobe came from, didn't you? The master bought them for young ladies he took a fancy to. Temporary adornment, you might say. So you see, there's no need to worry about Mrs. Scott-Ryan."

"You'd do anything Mrs. Rundle told you to, wouldn't you?"

"I expect so, miss." Katie tossed her head. "Yes, I would. So now you know."

"What hold has Mrs. Rundle got over you?"

"I've told you, miss. The workhouse. You've never been there, so you don't know."

If fear of it made Katie the kind of woman she was, I certainly did not want to know. To breathe a word of her disclosures would be to ostracize myself forever, as Katie well knew. I shivered at the thought of the long road and starvation.

To my surprise, the master announced that he wanted an inventory of the contents of the whole house.

"You're intelligent." His voice was grudging. "There's no one else who can do it."

"Is this what you brought me here for?"

"You jump very quickly to conclusions, miss. You're not here to ask questions. I give you a task, and you do it. Do you understand?"

I understood enough to know where my food and lodging were coming from. In fact, the project pleased me, and I set to work wholeheartedly.

I began by making a diagram of the house—the downstairs rooms, hall, passages and stairwells. I regarded the upstairs bedchambers as private and told the master so when I took the diagram to him.

He pursed his lips and gave me a calculating look. "If you consider it beyond you, I'll get Katie to do the whole of the confounded first story. She'll have no qualms about going into bedchambers."

I said with spirit, "As a servant, she's used to doing that. But I am not. I also have no authority.

He exploded. "Whose authority do you want? I'll have you know, miss, that *I'm* the authority here. What I say is paramount. Do you hear? Paramount!"

"I've never questioned your authority."

"Then get into the upstairs bedchambers!"

I remained defiant, determined not be be bullied by him. In the end, he pulled the bell sash and told Mary, who answered his summons, to send Katie to him. Several minutes later she came to the library door, bobbed and looked inquiringly from the master to me. When the master made his request, she bobbed again.

"Of course I'll do it, sir. I'll do the bedchambers while Miss Hannah does the downstairs." She paused and cast a veiled looked at me. "Do you wish me to do the tower rooms also, sir?"

"Leave the tower rooms to me," he thundered. "Be off with you, the two of you, and let me have the confounded lists by the end of the week."

"I shouldn't have asked," Katie murmured as we went out into the hall together. "It was such a good opportunity to get up there into the countess's rooms. I should have just gone up."

If you could get up, I almost said, but refrained just in time. The least said to Katie the better; personally, I had no desire to make the hazardous ascent merely to see an old woman installed in her bedchamber.

When the lists were completed, we took them to the master. After he had locked them away in his drawer, he motioned to Katie to remain, and I left the library feeling somewhat disgruntled.

I walked down the hall to the open side door and suddenly found my way blocked by Philip and Eton. With their return to Cambridge in two days, they seemed at loose ends. I had seldom seen them away from the dining table and was surprised to discover that they were quite tall. Indeed, rathe than giggling schoolboys, they carried themselves well and had the appearance of young gentlemen.

But as Philip set his foot in front of mine, I realized that his manners and behavior could belong to no one but a precocious schoolboy.

"So you regard yourself as a pretender, too," he sneered.

"What do you mean?" I asked quickly.

Instead of replying, he put his hand in his pocket and held up a golden object that I immediately recognized as my locket. I put out my hand to take it, but, tantalizingly, he held the locket behind his back.

"Where did you get that?" I demanded.

"Never you mind. You tell us why you're here, and we might let you have it."

"It's no business of yours," I retorted.

"It happens to be very much our business. My brother and I are male successors. You have no rights, pretender and all that you may claim to be. If the old countess fell out of her Bath chair on her birthday and broke her neck, it wouldn't be you who would succeed to Balaleigh. It would be I."

"Rubbish!" I tilted my head loftily. "Illegitimates have no legal rights."

"Pretenders. You've heard of James and Charles Edward Stuart, I suppose. This house once belonged to a Jacobite. I'm following in the footsteps of James, the old pretender; my brother, Eton, is the young pretender.''

"I don't care what you call yourselves. Neither of the Stuarts got anywhere, you know. As far as I'm concerned—and the world at large, for that matter—you're illegitimate. You might as well get going now. Neither of you has any rights to succeed to Balaleigh.''

"Do you think we're going to leave the way open for you?''

"It's no concern of mine what you intend to do. Will you kindly step aside and allow me to pass?''

"Don't you want the locket?'' Philip dangled it in front of my face.

"If I want it, I'll claim it—through the proper channels.''

"We'll tell our father you gave it to us,'' Eton put in.

"Tell him what you like.''

"Hoity-toity.'' Philip swung the locket around on its chain, and the force of the vibration sent it spinning from his hand and into a nearby rhododendron bush. "Now look what you've done! We'll tell our father that's all the care you take of the locket that belonged to his precious wife.''

I did not deign to look at him. But as I turned the corner, I saw the pair of them on their hands and knees, crawling under the rhododendron.

Katie knew nothing about the locket when I mentioned it to her. "You're sure it was the right one? she asked.

"As far as I could tell.''

She grimaced. "You need to be sure, if those urchins have anything to do with it. They're always trying to make trouble for someone."

When Philip and Eton departed for Cambridge two days later, I searched the ground under the rhododendron in vain. I despaired that I would ever see the locket again.

The one hundred and third birthday of the countess was now two days away. The kitchen was full of activity, and I understood from Mary that a variety of sweetmeats was being stored in white lolly bags in the kitchen.

"She throws them down from her Bath chair at the crowd. It's a grand sight, miss. You don't want to miss it."

"I'm sure no one will miss it," I replied, curious as to what kind of spectacle it was going to be.

That evening Richard came in too late for dinner, and unseen by the diners already at the table, beckoned to me from the dining-room door. I hastily excused myself under the pretext of a headache.

As soon as I emerged into the hall, Richard grasped my hand. "Is there a place where we can talk alone?"

"The cloakroom under the stairs."

He nodded. "Meet me in five minutes—inside the passage door."

I went up to my bedchamber, found the sal volatile and left it on the dressing table as proof that I had needed it for my headache. The family was eating dessert when I came downstairs. The hall fire was burning, but Dan was not about. I kept to the gloom cast by the furniture and made my way silently to the cloakroom door. At my knock the door opened immediately. Richard was standing behind it and drew me inside. He shut the door, then chucked me under the chin and kissed me. I gasped with surprise and said acidly, "I did not come here for that!"

He laughed. "It was too good an opportunity to miss, my dear Hannah."

"You forget Lady Caroline."

He grasped my shoulders. "Every time I meet you, you mention the lady."

"You must get used to that," I said more acidly still. "She is, after all, your betrothed."

His voice matched mine. "I didn't call you here to bandy words. You know what is happening the day after tomorrow?"

"Who doesn't?"

"What you don't know is that trouble is brewing. When the old countess comes down in that Bath chair, anything might happen."

"Why the sudden danger? The scaffolding that the workmen are erecting at the window looks strong enough."

"It is. There's no doubt about that. It's the soup kitchen at Matten that may have started the trouble. The peasants are hungry. I tried to persuade Scott-Ryan to do the same here, but he would have none of it. Keep away, Hannah. I don't want you hurt."

"But I want to see her," I protested. "I've heard so much about her."

"Keep away," he repeated. He took my hand. "Promise?"

"I—I—" But I never finished my sentence. He put his arm about my waist and tilted my head up. In the emotion of the moment I forgot my protests. I forgot Lady Caroline. As my mouth met his, I responded to his kiss in the manner in which it was offered. My emotions did not lie. I was still in love with him.

CHAPTER ELEVEN

The Bath Chair

I DID NOT KNOW what had come over me. In the secrecy of the dimly lit cloakroom, it seemed as though Richard and I had been in a world of our own. There was no master, no Mrs. Rundle, No Katie or Lady Caroline. We were alone with each other. Had I not responded to his kiss, I would not have felt so guilty afterward. But I had responded, in a way I had not believed possible, and we had clung together in a sudden realization that this feeling was greater than ourselves.

After he released me, he opened the cloakroom door and stood aside for me to go out. Then, without a word, he shut the door, and keeping to the shadows, went out the side door. I sauntered over to the hall fire and warmed my hands. I did not feel cold. My blood was still racing from the impact of his embrace.

The family came out of the dining room. Mrs. Scott-Ryan passed without even glancing at me, and the master went into the library. Philip and Eton, returned from Cambridge briefly for the birthday of the countess, stood giggling in the doorway. As they never took any more notice of me than Mrs. Scott-Ryan did, I was surprised when Philip approached me.

"Do you still want the locket?" he asked.

"I thought you'd lost it."

"Not I." He withdrew it from his pocket and twirled it in his hand. "How much is it worth?"

"Nothing, now that it's been in your possession."

"Or the pamphlet?" He produced that also.

"Let me see." I snatched it from him, opened it at the flyfleaf, which was blank, and returned it to him. "Where did you get that?"

"Ask Eton. He found it."

"I'm really not interested."

"You might be if you knew it concerned you."

I turned my back to him.

"Any stones fallen on you lately?" He started to giggle, and it occurred to me that I had heard the same inane giggling before, when the stone that missed me had struck forcibly into the ground.

I turned around and faced him. "Were you responsible for that?"

"I didn't say. I only asked a question."

"You seem to know all about the incident. What provoked it?"

"Tut, tut, Lady Hannah. We didn't throw the stone. It slipped. Why should we want to kill a fellow pretender? It fell, didn't it?" he asked Eton, who had joined him. "Why should we want to kill her when she's a pretender like ourselves?" They stood giggling and tittering together.

I decided they were nuisances, nothing more, although the stone they had apparently let fall could have killed me. How they had obtained the pamphlet I did not know. Since it did not have any writing on the flyleaf, I presumed the little book was not the one I had hidden in the library. I wished I could believe that the locket might not be the right one, either, but deep within me I knew that it was.

The next evening when Mary brought up my bath-water, I saw that she was wearing a locket. I regarded it circumspectly, because it was mine.

"Is that your locket?" I asked.

"No, miss. It belongs to my sister, Rose. She lost it, and Master Philip found it under the rhododendrons."

I made no comment. In the possession of others, the gold locket was like forbidden fruit, tantalizingly asking to be snatched at. Much as I wanted it back, I decided to bide my time.

Mary poured water from the ewer into the hipbath. "The old countess is coming down tomorrow morning, miss, at eleven o'clock. The master is keeping the gates locked until ten, and then he's allowing the people in. We always have a crowd on her birthday."

I wondered what kind of a spectacle would present itself on the morrow. I submitted to Mary's ministrations, which I much preferred to those of Katie, and soon was dressed in a old-rose brocade gown, tucked in at the waist and flowing out over the hips.

As I descended the staircase, I was surprised to see Lady Caroline sitting on the oak bench in the hall. She was wearing a blue silk gown, which, like mine, was tightened at the waist and had a full skirt. She smiled and appeared pleased to see me.

"Hannah, do sit down." She moved to make room for me on the bench. "It will give me great pleasure to converse with you until Richard appears."

I sat down beside her, murmuring, "You're a lady of quality. You're making rather much of a peasant girl."

"My dear Hannah, you're more than a peasant girl, and you know it."

I smiled wryly. "Fine clothes don't make a lady."

"Where did you get your clothes?"

"They were in the wardrobe when I came."

"Waiting for you?"

"Apparently. Katie, my maid, says they were made for a young lady of ordinary size, which does seem to explain why they fit so well."

"You're very fashionably and expensively gowned. Do you know why?"

"If I could answer that, I would know why I'm here."

"Don't you know?"

"No, indeed, I don't."

"Have you asked?"

"No one wants to enlighten me, least of all the master."

"He's a strange man. Have you consulted Richard?"

"Richard brought me here. He appears to know no more than I."

Lady Caroline toyed absently with her reticule. "You may think, Hannah, that I pass my days in trivialities. Nothing could be further from the truth."

I looked at her with some amazement. "I'm sure you do what you ought to do."

"I'm pleased to hear you use the word 'ought.' My life is ruled not so much by what I want to do as what I ought to do, or what I owe to others who are less fortunate. Richard says I'm foolish not to avail myself of opportunities for levity and social intercourse. He does not understand."

I grasped at the opening that Richard's name gave me. "Do you know Richard well?"

"We grew up together. He is my second cousin. His grandfather on the maternal side is a French émigré from the Great Revolution. Richard's family lost great lands and a magnificent château in the Loire Valley, which the Bourbon kings did nothing to restore when they came to power. Richard has built up a landed property in the colonies. A squatter, he calls himself. Whoever marries him will be expected to make her home in Australia." Lady Caroline shuddered. "A penal settlement—an outlandish kind of place by all accounts—but Richard loves it." Her sigh was scarcely audible.

"The year I came out, Richard returned from Australia for a short time. All the debutantes were agog for him, but their mamas looked the other way when they learned that the essence of the marriage contract was residence in Australia." Her face clouded. Her hands lay palms upward on her lap; the glitter of her diamond betrothal ring was hidden from view. Only the gold band visible on the third finger of her left hand showed that she was affianced. "Would it surprise you to know that Richard and I have very little in common? Oh, we hunt together, talk together, have similar family interests, but there it ends.''

"Lady Caroline, please don't go on," I begged.

"I need to. I must confide in someone close to my own age. Despite our class differences, I trust you, Hannah.''

I touched her arm. The silk of her sleeve was soft against my hand. My heart went out to her. I felt so sorry for her. She was a girl like myself, facing the doubts and fears of her own heart. I thought that I was in love with Richard, but I did not express my feelings. It appeared she very much doubted her own feelings for him, and the fact that I knew our emotions were centered on the same man made no difference to me. I did not feel insanely jealous, which made me wonder if I were truly in love with him. But this was tempered by the conviction that love did not exist between them, and so I could afford to be generous and sympathetic.

"What kind of a place is Australia?" I asked.

"Richard will tell you. He's obsessed with it, or possessed by it—I don't know which.''

"If you loved him, it wouldn't matter," I said softly.

"What do you know of love?''

"Enough to know that I couldn't marry without it.''

"What you don't realize are the other considerations—family, property, money. Family expectations, what is expected of oneself. I arrived late in my parents' marriage. Had I not come along, the property would have gone to Richard. Now I am the heiress to an estate my father still wants consolidated by marriage—preferably to Richard, who he believes, with marriage, will relinquish the hold Australia apparently has on him.''

"What do you really want?" I whispered. "If not Richard's love, what else?''

She smiled. "You probe well, Hannah, as you do most other things." She laid her hand on my knee. "When I was in London, I met a young gentlewoman who was my inspiration. I was impressed by the work she was doing with the poor in the little houses behind the Strand. After I spent some time with her, I realized that the poor of Ireland were crying out for help. England wouldn't heed their pleas. Well, you know what is happening at Matten House. Do you think I could leave that for an unknown place in a different hemisphere on the other side of the world?''

Suddenly fearful, I wondered if her good works would fade. But I managed to say, "Dear Lady Caroline, be guided by your own heart."

Mrs. Scott-Ryan and Mrs. Rundle were descending the staircase. Richard appeared from the side passage. Lady Caroline and I rose from the bench and became part of the group before the master appeared and the dinner gong sounded. During dinner, I had no opportunity to speak again either to Lady Caroline or to Richard, and as soon as good manners permitted, I retired to my bedchamber.

When day dawned, I got up early. I did not intend to leave my room. As soon as my toilet was finished, I asked Mary to bring me a breakfast tray. She looked surprised but did as I asked. I ate my breakfast sitting at the window, watching the tower. Stark and gaunt, it reached up into the sky with no sign of activity to relieve the austerity of its appearance. Its somberness was enhanced by the scaffolding especially erected at one of the tower windows. When Mary came back for the tray, she was astonished that I had made no attempt to don my shawl and bonnet.

"Surely you're going down, miss?" she asked.

"I can see very well where I am. It suits me to sit here by the window."

Grimacing, she tidied the room, made the bed and disappeared with the tray. I half expected Katie to come and escort me determinedly downstairs. But she did not appear, and after making myself comfortable at the window seat, I settled down to watch the proceedings.

At ten o'clock a drab procession of thin, ragged specters began to pour in. They raised their faces expectantly to the iron girder, cable and pulleys, which would lower the countess in her chair safely to the ground. While they waited, rain began to fall. With no shelter to accommodate them, they stood on the driveway getting thoroughly wet.

The countess was late, but at eleven-thirty, after the rain had stopped, the house bells began to ring. Balloons, released from the tower windows, floated out over the crowd. Then the window that was surrounded by scaffolding opened, and just inside I saw a huge, ornate, wheeled chair. I had read in advertisements about the self-propelled chairs that were made by James Heath of Bath for ladies and invalids and that were consequently known as Bath chairs. Hooded, elaborately painted and decorated, and attached to an iron girder by a cable, the chair was eased gently out of the window. It oscillated, but was steadied by pulleys, then came to a standstill in midair, only to be lowered slowly.

I saw an old woman, not as frail as I had expected, bonneted, caped and well strapped into the descending chair. Dressed in a gray gown of heavy brocade enlivened by rich multicolored threads, she stared down at the crowd and waved. But the drenched people did not cheer. They gaped. Someone called, "Buns, lolly cakes and pies!" Nothing was forthcoming, and a groan went up from hungry lips.

The master appeared on horseback with a crop in his hand. The countess began to throw small white lolly bags into the crowd. Some grasped at them eagerly; others waited to see what they contained. "Food!" the peasants cried. "Food for the hungry!" Those who caught and examined the contents of the lolly bags flung them contemptuously on the ground.

"Get going," the master thundered, brandishing his crop. Almost immediately the chair stopped in its downward movement and began to ascend. It watched it, my eyes glued to the occupant. The crowd began to stampede. The master's crop fell. Screams, not cheers, aggravated the chill air.

Richard appeared on horseback. He maneuvered his horse to the open gates and shouted, "Matten—go to Matten! The soup kitchen is open." The crowd jostled toward the gates, leaving behind a litter of white bags from which had fallen an assortment of sweetmeats that were now crushed into the sodden soil.

I watched until the Bath chair had disappeared
through the tower window and the crowd had dis-
persed to Matten. Then I went downstairs to the library. The house was deserted, so I had no qualms
that I might be watched. The pamphlet was still in the
place where I had put it. Even if it had been suppressed before distribution, some copies might have
escaped and could be elsewhere in the house. To sup-
press them all would be impossible, even if only a
small number had been printed. I did not begrudge
Philip his possession of one of them but was pleased
that no one had found and removed the library copy.

I was alone for the rest of the afternoon. Every now
and again I went to the library windows, which gave a
view of the tower. All was quiet. Apart from the scaffolding at the upper window, there was no evidence
that the countess had ever emerged in her Bath chair.

Dinner was late that evening, and the master was in
a surly mood. Richard ate his meal silently, then disappeared. I wondered how the peasants had fared at
Matten but dared not ask. My only hope was Richard. I had to see him. The longer I delayed, the more
urgent became my desire to speak to him. I wanted to
seek his assurance about an observation that was
causing me considerable alarm.

He was away for nearly a week, and I sat in my
bedchamber most of the time, watching the tower. At
night the lights blazed as usual, but otherwise there
was no sign of life. When eventually I did see Richard's carriage in the distance, I ran down to the front
door to wait for him.

He seemed pleased to see me, but his eyes were weary.

"What happened," I asked, "when the peasants reached Matten?"

"Nothing," he said. "Nothing at all. Lady Caroline was expecting them. The incident could have been nasty but for her. They were hungry and disappointed and in an ugly mood."

I pressed his arm. "Richard, I must speak to you. Now. It's urgent. I've been waiting for you—for days."

He smiled. "What is it?"

"Not here, please. I don't want to be overheard."

"Let's walk over to the keep," he suggested.

I walked beside him in silence.

"Well?" he prodded, looking at me half quizzically.

"It wasn't the old countess who was seated in that Bath chair!" I blurted out.

"What are you talking about?"

"I said it wasn't the countess."

"Do you know her?"

"No."

"How can you be so sure then?"

"It—it was someone else—someone I've met."

"Now you are being melodramatic. Who are you about to name, Hannah?"

"You're not taking me seriously."

"You're making a serious accusation. The whole world is assembled here at Balaleigh. The countess comes down from her hiding place in a Bath chair. She waves to the crowds and showers sweetmeats upon them. And what do you say? You say it wasn't the countess, after all! Whom do you think it was?"

"Old Maillard," I said. "It was old Maillard."

He stopped in his stride. "What makes you so sure?"

"I was watching from my window—you asked me not to go down—and I could see her very clearly. She wasn't as feeble as I expected a woman of her age to be. Her bonnet was too small. It didn't hide all her head. Her hair was thick and short, growing upright, straight out of the scalp. When I looked at her eyes—sea blue, not weak and watery—and her eyebrows—thick, gray and bushy—I knew it was no woman. It was old Maillard."

Richard walked ahead. I had difficulty in keeping up with him.

"Aren't you going to say something?" I almost sobbed. If our brief love encounters had meant anything at all, he had to believe me.

"I don't know what to say."

"You don't believe me, do you?"

"I don't *dis*believe you."

"Where was the old countess? Why didn't she show herself?"

He looked at me carefully, as if weighing his response. "At one hundred and three, would you feel like being hauled down from a tower in a Bath chair?"

"I'm not one hundred and three," I said petulantly.

"But the countess is. You forget, Maillard is her bodyguard. If Maillard were in the chair, he was there because she wished it."

I was not convinced. "You're keeping something back, I insisted. For some reason, he was not being frank with me. "Or do you think it's none of my business?"

His voice was level. "You live at Balaleigh. You have every right to be observant and draw your own conclusions." With a deft movement, he grasped my shoulders and touched his lips to mine.

"You cannot do this," I protested. "You are betrothed to Lady Caroline!"

"Betrothed but not in love."

"Are you trying to convince yourself?"

"Hannah, you're not being fair."

I said crossly, "I wish *you* wouldn't be so evasive."

He took my hands and kissed the palms. I felt the gesture was forced and put my hands behind me. He frowned, taken aback. "What made you do that? I was under the impression you liked to be kissed."

"I do—when the mood is sincere. At the present moment I'm not sure that your intentions are sincere. You're trying to cover up something."

"Come, Hannah, don't be absurd." He took hold of my wrist, but I twisted away from him.

"I came to you for help—advice—and this is the way you treat me." My voice broke.

"If you want my advice, forget the matter. Neither you nor I nor anyone else can undo what has been done." His tone was very deliberate.

"There's something wrong, isn't there? I can feel it in my bones."

He did not answer, and we walked back to the house in silence. I felt that Richard knew more about old

Maillard than he was prepared to say. I asked myself, what I really knew of Richard Ralston apart from his handsome appearance and a few surreptitious kisses. On the surface, he had come here with the purpose of finding a bride and taking her back to Australia. He had found his bride, but that did not stop him from kissing me. Was his love making merely a contrivance to divert my mind? Did he have something to hide?

I reached my conclusion swiftly and sharply. I would visit old Maillard at the first available opportunity.

CHAPTER TWELVE
Old Maillard

MY RESOLUTION was more easily resolved than solved. I had not counted on Katie. She watched me, lynx eyed. I could not guess her reason. Indeed, there seemed to be none.

Now she was wearing a pretty ring with sparkling diamonds on her betrothal finger, and she was happy. Only in the presence of Mrs. Rundle did she appear to be wilt. Since that breach between the master and his housekeeper was healed, they sought each other's company, a situation that did not appear to worry Katie. Betrothal to the master satisfied her, although it puzzled me why he would go to the extreme of marrying her. For Katie, marriage would sever her fear of Mrs. Rundle and the workhouse and would give her the material possessions she craved.

"You could have had him yourself if you'd tried," she told me one morning as she dipped my hairbrushes into a cleaning solution of hot water and soda.

"My ambitions never ran in that direction."

"The master is a much wealthier man than that Mr. Richard Ralston." Her eyes flashed triumphantly, and

I began to realize that Katie suffered from a burning ambition to become someone of consequence. She would do anything in her power to achieve this.

"Neither man interests me particularly," I said.

"Well, miss, the master's mine. I can't speak for Mr. Richard. However much he likes to flirt, I doubt if he's yours. Or anyone else's for that matter, despite his betrothal to Lady Caroline."

Katie was merely voicing my own opinion, but I offered no elaboration. "What do you know about old Maillard?" I asked.

"Nothing, miss."

"Don't you know why he's here at Balaleigh?"

"He's the countess's bodyguard. She needs someone to look after her, shut up in that tower day after day. If any ghosts rattled the doors, Maillard would soon frighten them away."

Realizing that there was nothing much to gain from Katie about old Maillard, I decided to hold my peace. Curiosity about the old man would merely draw attention to myself.

I was surprised that evening when Mary knocked hesitantly on my door. She had already brought up water for the hipbath, and I had not expected her to return so soon.

"I'm sorry to trouble you, miss," she muttered, "but Rose wants to see you." Behind Mary, I saw a tall girl whose resemblance to Mary plainly marked them both as sisters. I looked inquiringly at Rose.

"It's like this, miss," Rose began nervously. "My husband gave me a locket when we were courting, and I've looked after it ever since, until I lost it last month.

I didn't want to tell my husband, and Mary said to wait, as it might turn up. Well, it did, miss. Master Philip knew I'd lost it, and when he found it under the rhododendrons, he gave it to Mary. I thought it was my locket, miss—honest I did—but then I got it home and had a look at it, and I saw it was too big. I was going to get Mary to give it back to Master Philip when the back came loose—it was a fair-sized locket— and some papers fell out. Mary and I can't read, so we didn't know what name was on the papers. We stuffed them back into the locket and thought we'd return it to Master Philip. But he's gone back to school again, and we didn't want anyone to find a valuable locket like that on us. Mary remembered you'd lost a locket when you first came here, so we thought it might belong to you."

Rose thrust the locket into my hand. Much to my amazement, it opened to reveal some papers.

"You see what I mean, miss," Rose said, relieved. "The catch is loose. It opens easily. If you read the papers, you might find out who owns them."

I said as calmly as I could, "If you leave the locket here, Rose, I'll do so at the first opportunity."

After Mary and Rose had gone, I wrapped the locket and papers into a handkerchief and hid the bundle in a corner of the wardrobe. I promised myself to study the papers before I went to bed.

Dinner was dull. The master was suffering from an attack of gout and kept to his room, Philip and Eton had returned to Cambridge after the countess's birthday on May 6, and Richard was absent. Mrs. Scott-Ryan and I ate in silence. I could think of nothing to say and was surprised when she addressed me, looking directly at me and not above my head. "Have you any idea of Mr. Ralston's whereabouts?"

I shook my head. "I'm afraid I haven't."

"If you thought less about his kisses and more of his interests, you would serve Balaleigh much better," she remarked ungraciously.

"I don't regard myself as guardian of Mr. Ralston's movements," I said quickly. "Nor do I solicit his attentions."

She folded her table napkin. "Mrs. Rundle has a very different opinion, miss. Will you leave the table with me? I don't want you dining here alone with Mr. Ralston if he does happen to return."

"I've not finished my dessert," I protested.

She rose disdainfully. "It won't be wasted. The kitchen maids will consume it."

I got up and followed her out of the dining room.

"There is another matter, miss, to which I wish to draw your attention. You're far too free with the servants. For whatever reason the master brought you here, it was not to gossip with inferiors. Remember that in future. One minute a servant comes to me and says she has found your wretched locket; the next minute she says you've got it hidden in your bedchamber."

Stunned, I could not speak for a moment. But my rising indignation came to my aid. "The locket was brought to me with a request that I try to find out to whom it belonged. With that in mind, it is now in my possession."

"Bring it to my sitting room immediately."

"No, ma'am."

"So you intend to steal it!"

"I've no such intention. If the locket is mine, I will return it to the master."

"The master has nothing to do with it."

"Oh, yes, he has, ma'am. When I lost my locket, Mrs. Rundle gave it to the master. It has been in his possession ever since."

"Why is it now being passed around from hand to hand?"

"I don't know, ma'am."

"Regard yourself under suspicion until that locket is back in the place where it rightfully belongs." She swept majestically up the staircase. I did not follow her, but turned instead to study the portrait of the old countess.

A tired but patrician face looked back at me. The cheekbones were high, the lips thin. Determination pervaded the upright posture. I noted that the gown in the portrait was the same one in which the figure in the Bath chair had been clad. I looked closely at the gold locket hanging from a belcher-link neck chain. There was no doubt in my mind that this was the very locket Anna McCabe had thrust into my hand. And now it was in my wardrobe.

I stared long and hard at the painting. The countess's thin, lank hair, wrinkled face and sloping shoulders portrayed no evidence of the robust figure I had seen so recently in the Bath chair.

I returned to my bedchamber and retrieved the handkerchief bundle from the wardrobe, then withdrew the locket and its contents. One document re-

ferred to the marriage of Lady Berenice Balaleigh and
George Wellton, the third earl of Fullington. The second paper dated a year later was the birth certificate
of Lady Hannah Georgina Wellton. Myself!

I was neither overcome nor relieved. I felt exactly as
I had felt when I read the pamphlet and discovered
that Lady Berenice was my mother. Then I had
thought myself illegitimate. Now it appeared I was the
heiress to the Balaleigh estate. I was not a pretender.
When the old countess died, it was I who would le-
gally succeed.

Had the master opened the locket and read the papers? If he had, it was small wonder that he did not
wish to return the locket to me. Even now I trembled
at the thought of his reaction. My father must have
died shortly after my birth, for as detailed in the
pamphlet, my mother had married William Scott-
Ryan two years after I was born.

My thoughts flew to Richard. How much had he
known or guessed? Was that the reason for his attentions toward me—an attempt to ingratiate himself
with the future countess? I dismissed the idea as un-
worthy of him—and myself. He might be betrothed to
Lady Caroline, but he had set his sights on Australia.

What did Mrs. Rundle know? I recalled Katie's in-
sinuations after she had taken the locket from the
master's room. "It's all written on the paper inside the
locket." What Katie knew, Mrs. Rundle also knew.
My legitimacy could easily account for the housekeeper's desire to get rid of me.

And Mrs. Scott-Ryan? I did not believe she was
fully in Mrs. Rundle's confidence. She was merely a

dupe used by the housekeeper to consolidate her position with the master. Mrs. Scott-Ryan, wanting to legalize her own position with him, had feared a possible rival in myself. When my disinterest caused that fear to disappear, her dislike lingered. Although I felt she was well aware of my irregular birth, I doubted that she knew of this latest development.

Then there was Philip. If he knew the locket's secret, he would have kept quiet about it. In all probability, he had not been able to open the catch and had merely assumed that whatever the locket contained would verify my illegitimacy. Too much fiddling with the pendant had only weakened the spring so that it opened unexpectedly, not for him but for Rose, who could not read.

How could I prove that I was not an interloper intent on acquiring riches and a title? My strongest evidence was that I was myself—Hannah, taken from Balaleigh at seven years of age after the death of Lady Berenice, my mother, and sent to the cabin of Anna and Henry McCabe. Further proof of my identity lay in my possession of the locket, although Mrs. Rundle had insisted to the master that I had stolen it as a child. The most conclusive evidence, of course, was likeness to Lady Berenice, which had so upset Mrs. Rundle and Mrs. Scott-Ryan and which had been verified by the master himself.

Had he known all the time that I was the legitimate heiress, the next countess of Balaleigh? Was that why he had sent for me? Did he feel more secure with the rightful heiress, an insignificant girl whom he tried to dominate through fear, there on his threshold? Or was he biding his time for something else, something more sinister?

A tremor of fear shook my being as I made my decision. When the moment was opportune, I would confront the master with the issue.

I folded up the papers into the handkerchief, shut the locket and hid it in the wardrobe. Then I went silently downstairs to the library.

After making sure that the room was empty, I went to the shelves and withdrew the book in which I had hidden the pamphlet. When I had inserted the papers inside the lining on the back cover, I put the book back on the shelf and left the library.

I resolved once more to concentrate on old Maillard.

Watching the tower became an obsession. Each evening as dusk crept on, the lights glowed from the windows. Between midnight and one o'clock they were extinguished individually, as though someone, probably old Maillard, were going from room to room and story to story for that express purpose. I wondered at his agility in descending and ascending the crumbling staircase but remembered that the stairs near the wall were in fairly good order.

One afternoon, when no one was about, I judged the time was right to venture up the stairs to the tower.

The ascent was easier than I had anticipated. I discovered that by keeping to the safe side of the steps, I could grasp the small iron pegs probably inserted into the wall for this purpose. The tower was cold and musty. At the landing of each story, a little light filtered through stained-glass windows.

Breathlessly, I reached the top and began to open the surrounding doors. What I expected to find I did not know, but the rooms were the same as they had been before—empty, cold and unoccupied. If the old countess was really at Balaleigh, she was not living in the tower. Neither was old Maillard.

I could not guess who was responsible for lighting and extinguishing the lamps each night. I decided to retrace my footsteps and systematically search the two remaining stories of the tower. Despite my diligence, the result was the same. The countess and her body-guard were not here. Nor was there any trace of their residence in the rooms.

Deciding that I was merely wasting time here, I turned to go down when a sound startled me. Immediately I took refuge behind a door to one of the rooms. I heard heavy footsteps trudging up the stairs, followed by lighter ones. Huddled in my hiding place, my heart beating wildly and my body trembling, I peered through the eyehole in the door and saw Richard and old Maillard.

Richard wore a riding habit. Old Maillard, enveloped in a dark cloak, was carrying a small portmanteau.

"Are you sure you want to go?" Richard asked.

Maillard nodded. He was better dressed than when I had seen him previously in the tower, and his voice was less slurred. "The master has other plans. I can feel it in my bones. I'm not going to wait. He can't keep the old lady alive forever. Nature must take its course."

"It should have, long ago."

Maillard snorted. "He'll hold on to her as long as he dares. Are you coming with me, my boy?"

"No. I'll meet you in Cork. Stay at the Fleetfoot Inn. They know you're coming. Keep away from the brew and make no attempt to go on until I come."

"And you?"

"Unfinished business. Wait—and don't worry."

There was silence. I heard the lighter footsteps, which belonged to Richard, descending the stairs. But although I strained my ears, I could not hear the old man trudging after him. Where had Maillard gone? Rather than run into him by accident, I chose to remain where I was. The silence grew monotonous. Cramped behind the door, I grew stiff and impatient. I glanced around and could see the overcast sky through the window. Darkness was coming down quickly. I had to get back while the light lasted, but I dared not move.

I heard another sound and wondered if old Maillard had started to move. I saw a light coming upward, presumably from a lantern, and I heard humming. As the person passed the landing window, I was surprised to see that it was old Dan. Cautiously, on the safe side of the stairs, he was making his way to the top of the tower and lighting the oil lamps. Taking advantage of his concentration on his task, I tiptoed through the doorway and, pressing myself against the wall, began the descent.

Dan was no longer humming. But Maillard was not there; otherwise, Dan would have spoken to him. Where had Maillard gone? How had he left the tower?

THAT EVENING, dinner was normal again, with the master and Richard at the table. As usual, the meal was eaten in silence. But when Mrs. Scott-Ryan left the dining room and I followed her out, I felt Richard behind me. He tapped me playfully on the shoulder. "You owe me a kiss," he murmured in my ear.

"I owe you nothing," I retorted.

"The furze is blooming on the hills. Kissing is very much in fashion. What do you say, my sweet?"

"I'm not interested, is what I say."

He walked beside me down the hall, his voice low. "Would it interest you to know that I'm no longer betrothed to Lady Caroline?"

I stopped walking. Mrs. Scott-Ryan had gone up the stairway, so I could speak freely. "Has she seen you in your true colors? If so, I congratulate her."

"I don't understand, Hannah. Lady Caroline is a very strong personality, a fine personality. And rather than marry me and come to Australia, she prefers to devote her time to good works, particularly workhouse reform."

"Is that so?" Despite myself, my voice was cold.

He frowned. "There may be nothing between us yet, Hannah, but at least there's no obstacle—now."

"When are you going away?" I asked sharply.

He was taken aback. "What makes you think I'm going away?"

"Intuition," I said coolly. "Let's put it down to intuition. You say one thing and mean another."

We had reached the front door, which stood open to admit the fragrance of early evening. Richard paused, his eyes narrowed. "What reason have I given you to say that?"

"None—on the surface," I replied boldly. Then, fearful that I might say too much, I walked through the door and out onto the pavement. Water was flowing in the fountain, and a slight breeze stirred the leaves of a sycamore tree.

"I was in the tower this afternoon when you were saying good bye to old Maillard," I remarked casually.

"You were where?" He stared at me, stunned.

"In the tower."

"What were you doing there? You know that it's out of bounds."

"Not for me it isn't."

"What makes you so exceptional, may I ask?"

"I've a mind of my own."

"Hannah, do be reasonable!" He tried to take my hand, but I moved quickly aside. "Tell me, my dear girl, what took you there?"

"I went up to see the countess. Need I say how disappointed I was when I couldn't find her? Where is she, Richard? Do you know?"

He gestured impatiently. "Egad, how should I know?"

"Is she up there in the tower?"

"No."

"Is she dead?"

"Would you expect a one-hundred-and-three-year-old woman to be alive?"

"I suppose not. But it's possible, of course."

"Possible but not probable."

I moved restlessly. "Richard, please, can't you tell me the truth?"

"What truth is there to tell? She may be abroad, in Dublin, anywhere you name. It's just as easy to assume she's dead. Maillard has been masquerading for her long enough. It's unlikely that she's alive."

"So it *was* Maillard in the Bath chair!"

He nodded briefly.

"Richard, your words are not coming from your heart."

"Why should they, Hannah? I never knew the countess."

"She was a human being. She deserves some sort of reverence."

He took my wrist and held it so tightly that I cried out, "You're hurting me, Richard!"

"I beg your pardon." He sat down on the low stone wall surrounding the fountain and covered his face with his hands. "Maillard is my grandfather. I had no idea that he was masquerading as the countess until Lady Caroline wrote me that he might be a prisoner in the tower for that express purpose."

"Where did you think he was?"

"Here in residence—as a gentleman. It was a devilish thing to do to keep an old man prisoner for so many years!"

"He wasn't a prisoner," I said quickly.

Richard looked up at me. "What do you know about it?" he asked in surprise.

I recounted my experience in the dungeon. Richard listened, horrified, but I brushed his concern aside. "As you see, I survived with no harm done." He was silent for a moment. Then I asked, "Is that why you said you'd known Maillard all your life?"

"It was a way of evading your insistence, Hannah, that Maillard was performing a masquerade. When Lady Caroline wrote to me about it, I was completely taken aback. She had suspected something amiss for some time. I came to Balaleigh to investigate it, although the master did actually invite me when he knew I had business in Ireland. It didn't take me long to realize that I was dealing with unscrupulous people, so I worked quietly. I was aware of Scott-Ryan's motives. At all costs he must remain master of Balaleigh. It matters little to me what happens to the estate. In the absence of heirs, the Chancery is as good a body as any to administer justice. No one will be hurt. But while the countess is kept alive by a masquerade purely for the master's greed, my grandfather could be hurt— physically. I'm more concerned about him than anything else, so I'm taking him back to Australia. He didn't want to leave Balaleigh at first. He was quite satisfied with life in the tower and his secret way out into the hills to drink poteen. But I knew it was killing him—making him crazy."

"It's not only Maillard who's going crazy; it's all of them! Everyone at Balaleigh!"

"Maillard wasn't too crazy to realize that. After the last performance, he could see the dangers of the situation he was in. I persuaded him to leave."

"That was the best thing you could have done," I said. "What's going to happen here, now that he's gone?"

"The master must announce the death of the countess."

I shook my head. "He'll never do that. He's making plans to marry Katie, and when the famine's over—"

"The famine is worse. Everywhere people are dying, and those who are still alive are emigrating. It's worse than the master thinks, Hannah. Already he's suffered severe losses. There's no money to uphold the way of life at Balaleigh."

"What will happen to them all?"

"Devastation. A deserted house—you can find them all over the country. Decay everywhere. But in the master's case, it's worse. He's not the owner of Balaleigh. He won't have the title deeds—or the countess—to bring him back when the famine is over. He's no better off than the peasants he's evicted. The best thing he can do is try his fortunes elsewhere."

I gasped, recalling the conversation in the library between Richard and the master in which Richard had spoken of gold in New South Wales.

"Not Australia?" I whispered.

"Why not, my love?"

"I don't like him," I said stubbornly, scarcely conscious of what my words implied.

Richard got up and stood beside me, raising my head and kissing me. "Australia's full of such people, dear Hannah. It's a vast, lonely country. The strong survive and the weak go under. We can't choose our neighbors under the Southern Cross. We're grateful to have them."

"I'm sure *I* don't want to choose neighbors," I said decisively. "In fact, I've no intention of doing so. Good night."

"Hannah!"

But I turned and walked away from him, then ran through the open door, past the portrait of the countess and up the great staircase.

He did not follow me, nor did I expect him to.

Once in my bedchamber, I sat at the window and gazed at the tower. The lights were blazing at the windows. I sat for a long time, waiting and watching. Silhouetted against the night sky, the tower presented a picture of formal domesticity. The countess was at home. Then, as midnight approached, the lights began to go out. Soon the tower was shrouded in darkness. To all intents and purposes, the countess had retired for the night.

CHAPTER THIRTEEN

The Proposal

RICHARD HAD NOT elaborated on his relationship with old Maillard, and I had not asked any questions. If Richard wished to add anything to his admission, he would do so in his own time. The important thing now was the master's reaction to Maillard's escape and his inevitable acceptance of the death of the countess. With that must come the realization of his monetary straits and his vacating of Balaleigh, both of which would mark the death knell to his scheming.

I dared not think of my own future.

The disappearance of Maillard was not mentioned, nor would it be, since he had been a virtual prisoner in the tower. Richard remained at Balaleigh, but I heard no speculation as to his departure. He continued to manage the estate with, I thought, increased energy.

One afternoon, the master sent for me. Somewhat tremulously, I knocked on the study door and entered, wondering what he had in mind. The study was a small book-lined room leading from the library. Mrs. Scott-Ryan was seated in an armchair before the fire. The master, his feet resting on a stool, lowered his newspaper as I crossed the room. I was not invited to sit down but stood facing them both.

By way of preamble, the master cleared his throat. "What have you done with the locket?" he demanded.

Not altogether taken by surprise, I withdrew it from my pocket and placed it on a small table near him.

A malicious expression crossed Mrs. Scott-Ryan's face. "What did I tell you?" she cried. "She had it all the time, the nasty little thief!"

The master frowned at her. "One thing at a time, my good woman." He addressed me. "Is that the locket you purported to claim as yours?"

"It is the locket Anna McCabe gave me as a parting gift." I faced him steadfastly.

"The locket that *I* kept in my possession. Can you explain how it came into your hands?"

I chose my words carefully. "One of the servants lost a locket. Master Philip found one beneath a rhododendron bush and gave it to her, thinking it was hers. When she realized it was not, she brought it to me, knowing that I had lost my locket when I first came here."

I could not be sure whether the master accepted my statement. He appeared to be in a quandary. He picked up the locket and held it between his thumb and forefinger. I decided to take the initiative. "May I have the locket, please?"

He stared. "No!" The locket is valuable. It has not only sentimental value but a place here in our family archives. This locket was worn by the countess of Balaleigh when her portrait was painted. It has never been in the possession of a peasant. How it came into

your hands was the result of a neat contrivance by
Anna McCabe. This is the last I want to hear of the
matter. It is ended."

I shut my mouth on words of righteous indignation. I needed time to think. If the master knew the
secret of the locket, argument would be fruitless. But
did he? I decided to question the point of my sojourn
at Balaleigh. "When am I to be given the duties for
which I was brought here?"

Instead of raising his voice as I had expected, he
looked at me intently. "I can see, miss, that you need
to be occupied. That is the only way to keep you out
of mischief. I will send Katie to you very soon. Be
prepared for what I regard as a serious task." He
turned to Mrs. Scott-Ryan. Feeling myself dismissed,
I curtsied and left the study.

I was not altogether happy about Katie's inclusion
in whatever my new duties would entail. I would have
preferred to deal directly with the master, acting without assistance.

Not knowing what to do with myself in the mean-
time, I walked down to the stables. But Tom was ex-
ercising the horses in the far field, so I turned
dejectedly away, only to hear Richard's voice hail me.
"Hannah, you're the very person I wanted to see!"

He reined in his horse beside the stalls and dismounted as the stableboy took the bridle. He looked
very handsome with the sun shining on his dark hair
and on his brown, well-cut riding coat, enlivened at
the neckline by a red silk cravat.

"Let's go for a walk," he suggested.

I agreed willingly enough, thinking that his company was better than none. But it seemed as though my emotions with regard to him had ceased to exist. Try as I might, I could not feel the elation that I had once experienced in his presence. My senses were numbed. But I was aware that he regarded me quizzically.

"I'm courting you, Hannah," he said as we crossed the gravel to the track that led up the hillside behind Balaleigh.

"What if I don't want to be courted?" Despite myself, I felt my numbed senses quickening, and peering at him from beneath my lashes, I knew that I was still in love with him.

His voice was cheerful. "There are always ways of overcoming opposition." He took my hand, and I trembled, anticipating his kiss. But he did not attempt to kiss me. Instead, he quickened his pace, pulling me along with him.

"I know very little about you other than what I see at Balaleigh," I said.

"Isn't that enough?" He pressed my hand playfully.

"No, it is not. You may be an adventurer for all I know, living here on the master's goodwill."

"Is that the impression you have of me?" He let go of my hand.

"I—I don't know," I faltered.

"For your information, Miss Hannah McCabe, I emigrated to Australia some years ago. I am what is known as a squatter, a man who owns and rules his land with the cooperation of the government. My station—that is the name we give to big farms—consists of many thousands of acres of good grazing land, situated two hundred miles west of Melbourne in what is known as the Port Philip District.''

"Was it your only grandfather who brought you back to Ireland?''

His smile was disarming, and again he took my hand. ''I need a wife.''

"What was wrong with the women out there?''

"One likes to be selective not only in sheep but in women, too.''

My face flushed. "I don't mean to be inquisitive, but I must know your real interest in Balaleigh.''

"You do know, Hannah. It's my grandfather.''

"But you just said—''

"That I wanted a wife.'' He chucked my chin. "So I do, my dear. A tender, loving wife who commands both my respect and my love. *All* my love. I'm not deriding Lady Caroline when I say that. Ours was a childhood courtship that, unfortunately, had no fruition—for either of us. If our courtship is to be successful, Hannah, it would mean your leaving Balaleigh.''

Although gasping for breath at the turn the conversation had taken, I managed to say, "Balaleigh is not the entire world.''

He stopped walking. His eyes searched my face and held mine in a long, questioning look. "It would mean going to the other side of the world—twelve thousand miles to Australia.''

Much to my surprise, I found myself asking, "What's so terrible about that?''

"You may not like it.''

"Would you ask me if you thought I wouldn't?"

"I don't know." His hands hung at his sides. "I love you, Hannah. If I could convince you of that, would you come?"

"What is it like, this place called Australia?"

"Like nothing you can visualize, my love. It's vast, raw, heartless. You either survive or go under. If you survive, you put something of yourself into the soil that you can't take away. It holds you to it, in a voracious embrace. At the same time, it gives you nothing unless you slog for it with your life's blood. It possesses you."

"It might possess me, too."

"Do you want to be possessed?"

"I don't know. I truly don't know." I trembled, not with fear but with uncertainty. The suddenness of his proposal overwhelmed me. "Please, please, Richard, give me time to think. I need time. Things are crowding in on me."

"What manner of things?"

"I don't know. The master has something in mind. He brought me here for some reason. He—he's going to send Katie to me in a few minutes and give me a 'serious task,' he said."

Richard's hand gripped mine. "Should you need me, I'm here, Hannah. Remember that." He brushed his lips over mine, and we turned back toward the stables.

Did I love him enough to trust him not only with my future but with my life? I sighed, not really knowing the answer but hoping that soon I would.

When I entered the house, Katie was waiting for me at the head of the staircase. "I've been looking for you everywhere, miss. The master said to bring you now."

"What does he want?"

She shrugged. "Only he knows. He wants us to go up there." She nodded toward the tower stairs.

"Into the tower?"

"Yes, miss."

"But the stairs aren't safe. He's forbidden anyone to use them."

"They're safe enough, miss, and well he knows it. Tread carefully and slowly. You won't come to any harm."

I followed her, feigning unfamiliarity with the stairs. But Katie was sure of her way and every now and again turned to see if I was safe. "Keep to the left, miss, and use the pegs in the wall." I did as I was bidden, and we reached the first landing.

"Do you come here often?" I asked as we paused for breath.

"I used to, miss, when I was little. I loved climbing up to the tower to see how high I could get."

We reached the top of the stairs and scrambled onto the landing. The master's voice came to us from within the tower room.

"Come in and shut the door," he ordered.

We did so. But once inside, I had the horrifying feeling that I was in a trap. The master was not alone. Mrs. Rundle was with him. She approached me and, to my amazement, began to remove my gown from me. She was a strong woman against whom I found it impossible to struggle. Katie slipped another gown over my head. The lining felt soft, like silk, but the gown itself was of heavy brocade. It smelled musty and was, I suspected, not too clean. I recognized it as the gray gown that old Maillard had worn in the Bath chair. My shoes were pulled off and boots were put on my feet. Then came the wig, huge and tawny, which fitted on my head like a grotesque cap.

"Sit down in the Bath chair," Mrs. Rundle ordered. When I hesitated, she and Katie seized me by the arms and pushed me into the commodious chair. I glanced apprehensively at the stained-glass window, fearing that at any minute I might be wheeled toward it and lowered to the ground, but no scaffolding was visible.

"Now the locket." Mrs. Rundle placed it around my neck, then paused and withdrew it. She fiddled with the clasp. The back of the locket sprang open. It was empty. Nonplussed, she turned angrily to the master. "There's nothing there. Did you remove them?"

"What, my love?"

"The papers hidden in the locket. They're gone."

"I haven't seen them, my dear."

Mrs. Rundle pointed a finger at me accusingly. "Did you force the locket open and remove the papers? Family papers, belonging to Balaleigh. Answer me, miss. Don't sit there staring."

"I know nothing about them," I said petulantly.

She turned to Katie. "Didn't you see papers in the locket?"

"Yes, ma'am," Katie said.

Mrs. Rundle was in a rage. "The locket was in your possession, miss! You opened it!"

I replied calmly, "It would not open."

"So you tried?"

"Of course I tried."

"Well?" She folded her arms threateningly. At any moment I expected her hand to fly out and hit me on the face. "You're lying."

I was silent, eyeing the locket, which she put in her pocket.

"She needs to be punished." The housekeeper moved to grasp the master's walking stick, but he forestalled her.

"Leave her," he said. "Katie, lead the way down the stairs." He offered his arm to Mrs. Rundle. Like characters in a play, they walked to the door. I tried to rise, but the long heavy gown, the narrowness of the chair and the cumbersome wig impeded my movements. Katie stood at the door, waiting until the master and Mrs. Rundle passed through. Then she slammed it in my face and turned the key in the lock.

I was alone in the tower retreat of the countess of Balaleigh. For the first time I realized that Mrs. Rundle had not returned the locket. She had put it in her pocket. What to do next? My clothes were gone. Katie had thrown them out of the room as soon as Mrs. Rundle had removed them from me.

The tower room lacked air. The sun, shining through the stained-glass window, warmed my body. Despite the discomfort of the huge chair, my head nodded, and I fell asleep. When I awoke, the sun was setting. I saw my reflection in the opposite window. I was an old woman sitting in a chair, not humped but upright and bewigged. But I was not anonymous.

Here in the tower I had an identity. I was the countess of Balaleigh.

I took off the wig. I could not remove the heavy brocade gown, for there was no other in the wardrobe. But at least I could undo the buttons. Feeling more comfortable, I sat down on the settee and watched the moon rise. Long shadows stretched out in the room. The silence was eerie. I looked across the stone pavement and saw the old keep rising, broken yet majestic, into the dark sky.

And suddenly I knew that I was a prisoner. I was at the mercy of the inhabitants of Balaleigh. I clutched my hands in despair. For how long would my existence continue like this?

I was without food until Katie brought me some bread and milk at midday. After entering, she left the door unlocked and placed the bowl on the dressing table. She eyed me mockingly, but her manner lacked the spite she had displayed when Mrs. Rundle was present. "I see you've tidied up the place."

"With nothing else to do, it was the obvious solution," I said acidly. "The room smelled. It still does. If you must leave me here, can't you put me somewhere else?" My eyes were on the door.

"Don't try it," Katie said, backing toward the entrance. "Old Dan is on the landing, trimming the wicks of the lamps, and the master isn't far away." She sniffed the air and turned down her mouth. "She was an old slut," Katie said with feeling.

"Who?"

"The countess, of course."

"Katie," I said, "don't try to deceive me. When did the countess die?"

She looked surprised. "So you know."

"It wasn't difficult to deduce. When, Katie?"

"Years ago—shortly after Lady Berenice married the master. Her death was kept quiet."

"Was the marriage too much for the old lady?"

"She arranged it. She didn't want to see her granddaughter husbandless and the child fatherless. Yes, Lady Berenice had a child."

I said sharply, "I'm not discussing Lady Berenice. I'm talking about the countess."

Katie sat down in the Bath chair. "What do you want to know?"

"What my impersonation of her implies."

"Why not ask the master?"

"Why not say Mrs. Rundle?"

"Oh, well." Katie shook her fair hair over her face and began to plait a long strand. "I know he's at her beck and call. What can I do?" She rose suddenly. "I've got myself to look after."

"Of course. But I'm not discussing you—or them. I'm talking of the countess. What am I expected to do?"

"Do what old Maillard did. Impersonate her. He did very well all these years, for all that he drank his brew when the countess was supposed to be away."

"Was he a prisoner?"

"Most of the time."

"Did he ever get out?"

"He must have done so when the master forgot to lock the door. We'd find him miles away. But when the famine came, he didn't wander much. Now Mr. Richard is taking him back to Australia. That's why he came here—to do that and get a wife. That sneaky Lady Caroline used to poke around Balaleigh when he was away. She must have written him that she thought his grandfather was imprisoned in the tower to masquerade as the countess. Mr. Richard had to know some way. Back he came in a towering rage. Not that the master cared. Maillard's out of the way, and the master sent for you—to act as the countess for as long as the master lives."

I walked across to the window. "Katie, will you do something for me?"

"It depends."

"Fetch a book from the library. I'll go mad sitting up here all day doing nothing."

"Which book?"

"The one on the third shelf next to the door. A big blue book called *The History of European Art*."

"Lawks-a-mussy, miss, what next? How do you expect me to remember that?"

"It's got pictures—colored pictures. It will be something for me to look at."

"I'll think about it. I'm not used to books."

"Can you read?"

"Yes."

"The big blue book, on the third shelf next to the door. *The History of European Art*."

"I won't promise," she said. She took the key out of her pocket and inserted it into the outside of the lock. "That will make sure I don't forget to lock you in. On high days and holidays you'll get into that old chair, miss. It's taken to the window and lowered to the ground. You've seen it. When the people cheer, you'll throw them peanuts and lollies and look hideous. And everyone will say, 'How much longer will she last?' You're one hundred and three years old, miss, and you've got to keep going until the master dies. He's not a young man, but he's not that old, either. Now you know what's expected of you.''

She walked through the door and slammed it after her. I heard her turn the key in the lock.

CHAPTER FOURTEEN

Prisoner

THIS WAS WHY the master had agreed to Anna Mc-Cabe's request that I should come to Balaleigh. Unbeknownst to Anna but to suit his ends, he had brought me here to masquerade as the countess for the rest of his life.

That night I dreamed that I was descending from the tower in the Bath chair. I was looking down at scores of hungry peasants who were raising their faces to me and begging for food. All I could give them were peanuts. I threw them out into the crowd until the master came and brandished his walking stick. The peasants trampled the shells into the ground and disappeared. I was left alone, suspended in midair in the Bath chair while the wind played mercilessly with my caplike wig. Just when Richard came, I awoke.

It was morning. The light was coming in through the window. I turned over and tried to continue the dream but could not. I lay on my back, staring at the ceiling. What was I to do with myself during another long day? I got up, made the bed and tidied the room. Katie had left some water in the ewer on the washstand. I washed my face and covered my arms in the refreshing water. When I was dressed, I sat on the settee and waited.

What I was waiting for, I did not know. Meals were spasmodic, and no visitors came. After the dream, my mind was filled with Richard. I needed to see him. But how could he guess where I was unless Katie, in an unguarded moment, let slip my whereabouts? My head whirled. I could seek no answer to my dilemma from the four walls of my solitude.

I heard someone mounting the stairs and walking along the landing. Footsteps stopped at the door of the room. I heard the jangle of keys, and then the door opened. The elfinlike face of Dan was peering in at me.

He touched his forelock, recognizing me despite my grotesque attire. "Old Maillard not here, miss?"

"He's gone," I said.

"Are you taking his place, miss?"

"What makes you say that?"

"They locked old Maillard up here when they said he must masquerade as the countess. Not that he minded, as long as he had his brew and his own secret way of getting out. After a while they didn't even bother to lock the door. They knew he was dependent upon them."

"What was his secret way?" I asked.

Dan winked. "Old Maillard's secret. Not mine." He put out the oil lamp. "I come up here every morning and night to do the lamps. The old countess is still supposed to be in residence. That's what the master says. He's spreading abroad that she never went back nowhere after her birthday on May the sixth. Just stayed here. 'Must keep the lamps alight,' he says. 'The old countess can't live in darkness. People must know she's still there. What better way to let them know than to keep the lamps burning?' So you see, miss, I'll come up every night and morning.''

"Do you bring food with you?''

"No, miss. Are you hungry?''

I nodded miserably.

"Old Dan will see what he can do. We won't say naught to anyone. I'll just bring you a mouthful or two.''

"Dan,'' I pleaded. "Dan, will you let me out?''

"Can't, miss.''

"Why not?''

"Not till the master dies.''

"The master could live forever.''

"Aye, that he could.''

I edged to the door, but he forestalled me. "No good, miss. They're watching. You'd never get far down the stairs.'' He came close to me and whispered, "What would you do, anyway, if you got out there? The roads are full of souls like you, not knowing where to turn next, lying down on the roadside and eating grass, dying. You don't see them here, miss, but they're out there. Don't join them. Stay here, and old Dan will get you a mouthful or two.''

"How long has the countess been dead?''

He scratched his head. "Fifteen years or more it was since the fire went out in the hall. Aye, fifteen years or more when old Maillard first came to Balaleigh. A French aristocrat he was, beggared by the Great Revolution. The old countess took him in. She had more than a soft spot for him, aye, more than a soft spot. His son, Mr. Richard's father, emigrated to Australia when Mr. Richard was born. But old Maillard was at Balaleigh, and when the countess died, the master said, 'He can masquerade as her.' She looked and acted like a man, miss, in her declining years. The night the fire went out in the hall, they took her body out to sea and buried her.''

''Who?''

''Those that got old Maillard; now they've got you.''

Aghast, I stared at him. ''Was he here all that time?''

''Until Lady Caroline stumbled upon him in one of his wanderings in the village and let Mr. Richard know. Then back he comes from Australia, like a cork popping from a bottle, to take his grandfather back with him. Not that old Maillard wanted to go. But if he's gone, miss, he's gone. Mr. Richard will see that he doesn't come back. And now you're here, taking his place. You'll be old when the master dies—too old to want to get out.''

''Dan,'' I said. ''Dan!'' But he did not reply. He left the room, locking the door behind him.

I sat on the settee and stared ahead of me. I saw the the wardrobe against the wall, the window bereft of curtains and blind, the bed with its stale-smelling bedclothes and the washstand. I had read of prisoners counting the hairs of their heads. I sat and did nothing. There was nothing to do.

The sun shone through the window. It warmed me, and I felt sleepy. But I knew that if I slept, I would not sleep during the night.

So I continued to sit, fighting sleep.

I recited poetry. I counted to a thousand, then backward to one. I tried to remember Euclid. It was not hard to draw triangles, oblongs and rectangles on the dusty wardrobe door.

Would Richard try to seek me out, or was he too intent on getting his grandfather to Australia? Would Lady Caroline miss me? What story would the master fabricate? It was true that he was not young. Nor was he old. He had no intention of allowing Balaleigh to slip from his grasp during his lifetime.

I longed for Katie to come. I longed for her to bring the book. But nothing disturbed the silence of my prison.

I thought I would go mad. I was hungry, but no subsistence came for either my body or my mind.

That night I undressed and tossed on the bed. I got up and remade it, and slipping again between the blankets, fell into dreamless sleep.

Katie woke me in the morning. She was standing by the side of the bed, looking down at me.

I sat up, rubbing my eyes. "Did you bring the book?"

"I brought food." She produced some stale bread and a bottle of water.

"The book, Katie, where is the book?"

"I couldn't find it, miss."

"Of course you found it. You were too curious not to find it. Why didn't you bring it?"

"There was no need to. I found these." She rummaged in her pocket and produced the papers I had hidden in the covers of the book. "I brought this, too." She put the pamphlet on the bed.

"And read them all," I said.

"Yes, miss. Or should I say my lady?"

"It makes no difference—here."

"I'm sorry, miss. A fine ladyship you would make. I mean that. It's a pity it can't be."

I made no reply. I was wondering what to do with the papers when Katie produced the locket and dangled it before my eyes.

"Where did you get that?" I asked, startled.

"From the Balaleigh archives—in the study leading from the library. When Mrs. Rundle returned it, I saw the master lock it in a cabinet. I thought it was more appropriate for you to have it, to protect the papers, you know. I knew where he kept the key, so I got the locket out."

"Will he miss it?"

"What does it matter if he does? He won't suspect either of us. You can hardly steal a locket from here and I—well—" She shrugged. "I'd hardly be interested in it."

Silently, I took the locket, returned the papers to its safety and put it around my neck beneath my gown.

"That's better. Now we can forget about it." Katie went toward the door. "I don't know when I'll be back, miss."

"I've got to eat," I said. "I can't live on bread and water."

"I know, miss. There's some talk about having you downstairs. Now that you know what's expected of you, you're almost one of the family. It isn't really necessary to stay here all the time—that is, as long as you're not planning to run away."

I extended my hands helplessly. "Where would I run?"

"Yes, miss. Where would you run?" She went outside and locked the door.

The next few weeks were a nightmare that I never cared to think about afterward. Meals were brought to me spasmodically by either Katie or Dan, but mostly by Dan. He brought them in the mornings and evenings when he came to attend to the lamps. I looked forward to the meals, as they were the chief diversion of my day, and tried to keep the room and myself as neat as possible.

After what seemed an endless seclusion, I heard someone fumbling at the door lock shortly after I had finished my evening meal. The door opened to reveal the master. He looked unkempt and was breathing heavily. I could see that he had been drinking.

"Coming up those stairs deserves a reward," he said, advancing into the room toward me.

I backed to the window.

"One kiss," he said. "That's all I want. One kiss."

"You're drunk," I cried, trying to fend him off with my hands.

"Bah! Not too drunk to know what I want. That precious Richard Ralston comes back from Australia to see how I'm treating his grandfather. Special rooms I'd given the old man up here in the tower and security for life in return for small jobs he did for me. But was Mr. Richard satisfied? Not he. Back he's taking Maillard to Australia. I intended to have you to take Maillard's place, but now I've got a better idea. I plan to marry you."

"What!" Instead of backing away from him, I stood at my full height, cumbersome in the countess's gown. "You can't marry me!"

Perspiring profusely, he leered at me. "Why not, pray?"

"You can't marry your stepdaughter."

His laughter was raucous. "You think you're my stepdaughter, do you?"

"I have proof."

"If you're talking about the pamphlet, it was suppressed before publication. Suppressed, do you hear?" His tongue lolled. Saliva drenched his chin.

"So it was you who wrote that on the flyleaf, not Mrs. Rundle."

"Egad, you were paying too much attention to it— in the library every day, making notes." He caught his head in his hands and swayed. I thought he was about to have a seizure.

I sat down on the settee and announced as calmly as I could, "I am the daughter of Lady Berenice Balaleigh, who married George Wellton, the third earl of Fullington. I am not an illegitimate daughter but a legitimate daughter."

"What's that? Legitimate! You?" He pointed a wobbling finger at me. "Don't tell me lies. Being here alone is making you insane!"

"I've proof," I said.

"Bah! Who's to believe you? Despite everything, I'll marry you. Yes, I'll marry you. A peasant bride. That will suit my purposes admirably." He rubbed his gnarled hands in anticipation.

I gulped. "The church forbids it."

He ignored me. "As my wife, your duty will be to masquerade as the countess. I need not keep you prisoner here and climb these damnable stairs to enjoy you. I should have thought of it before—indeed I should." He came toward me. His hands clutched my body. "Remove this confounded gown and show yourself for what you are. A plumper wench than Katie, for all that she gives herself airs. No need now to announce the death of the countess. May she live forever, the dastardly woman, while I have a marriage of convenience and keep Katie, as well." He slapped his thigh and guffawed. "Prepare yourself, Miss Hannah, for tomorrow we wed."

"I'll need time," I said, suffering his caress, but at the same time edging toward the window. I maneuvered myself behind the Bath chair. "Just give me time."

His mouth slobbered on my face and neck. "Why do you want time?"

"To make plans for the wedding. Every young lady needs time for that. Surely a man like you, the master of Balaleigh, would not begrudge me that."

"How much time?"

"Two days."

"All this fuss to marry a pauper," he mumbled. "An illegitimate pauper." I was silent. If he knew the truth about my birth, he was not going to admit it.

Astute enough to know that he could not marry his stepdaughter, he preferred to profess ignorance and go ahead with the marriage.

Scott-Ryan walked to the door and fumbled with the key. It was no use my trying to push him and dodge outside. He was too heavy, and it would antagonize him. Furthermore, where would I run with others watching and waiting on the stairs? He put the key in the lock. "Once you're married to me, you won't escape."

"I wouldn't expect to," I said.

When I was sure that he had gone, I looked wildly about the room. I had to get away. But how? I began to panic. If there had been another and easier way of descent, old Maillard would have used it. He had come out of a pit of darkness into a dungeon. I had seen him. He was used to such a practice. Not for him the main stairway, where he might be perceived.

The story of the master forgetting to lock the door was a mere fable. Maillard had not cared if the door was locked or not. He had his own special way of getting out.

"Where?" I cried out. "Where?"

I tore at the bedclothes. They were rotting. Three or four strips plaited together would give them strength, but not safety to me. I despaired and ran to the window. The June night stared back at me. I could see the ground far below. How could I reach it without endangering myself?

It began to rain. I heard the drips on the windowpane. I retreated to the far corner and opened the huge wardrobe. The sound of rain did not cease. I could still hear it somewhere in the wardrobe, yet the wardrobe was dry.

I walked inside it. The toe of my shoe caught at an iron ring in the floor. I stooped down, caught the ring in my finger and, rising slightly, pulled it. The floor moved. I saw the outline of a movable square, and I pulled harder. The wardrobe floor started to lift. A hollow square opened wide to reveal a gaping depth. Rain was dripping in the gloom beneath. And then I saw the stone steps cut into the thickness of the tower wall.

I cried out with joy. I could escape. The means was here. I did not need to climb down rotting bedclothes and hope that I would reach the ground safely. I could walk down—if I kept my head and was not afraid.

I descended three steps. They were solid, and I decided to go on. I did not pull the trap door shut. If the steps led nowhere, I must return. On the other hand, if either Dan or Katie did not see me in the room in the morning, it would not take the master long to find my escape route. But I had to take some risks, and I judged I would be far away when his ire was aroused.

The steps led to a long, dark tunnel. I went on slowly, choosing my steps carefully and staring at a small ball of light that was steering me in a straight line to whatever lay ahead. I walked steadily, my heart beating fast but my mind alert. The walls were damp; it was wet underfoot, and at intervals I could hear water dripping. I longed for the light to grow bigger, which would indicate that I was at the opening of the tunnel. But instead of enlarging, the light began to recede, and I lost it altogether.

I groped my way along the wall of the dark tunnel. After what seemed endless minutes, I stubbed my toe against an immovable object. The sharp impact caused me to wince. I bent down to see what it was and in the gloom made out ascending stone steps. Then the overhead darkness lightened, and I left the top step to enter a room bathed in moonlight.

I recognized it immediately. I had come along an escape route and up the cesspool into the old keep. I had trodden the way of old Maillard and countless others who in the past years had sought to escape from Balaleigh. I picked my way across the rubble to the wooden door. If it was locked, I would be undone. But it was not. It moved to my urgent pressure, and in another moment I was outside.

I gasped with relief and drew the fresh air deep into my lungs. To my right was Balaleigh, gray, silent and ghostlike in the moonlight. I saw the tower, tall and gaunt, from which I had escaped. The lights were still shining in the windows. The escape route had led me beneath the pavement and into the heart of the old keep. In all probability it had been an escape tunnel when the family had combated the Jacobites and, later, Oliver Cromwell.

On the far side of the keep from Balaleigh, I made myself as comfortable as I could on some smooth boulders. I dared not sleep. Indeed I had no desire to do so. So great was my relief to be free of my prison that I merely sat and stared at the space around me. Despite myself, I must have dozed, for I was suddenly conscious that the sky was brightening. Dawn was coming over Balaleigh.

Soon old Dan would put out the lights in the tower. He might or might not notice my escape. But eventually the alarm would be raised and the trapdoor in the old wardrobe discovered. I would be pursued. The master, emerging from his drunken stupor, might not remember his proposal of the night before. But most certainly, at the first hint of my escape, he would climb the tower stairs to investigate.

What to do? Where to go? I hurried along, making my way as inconspicuously as possible among the hedgerows that divided the deserted fields. What had old Maillard done? How had he survived? For it was not recapture that obsessed my mind with fear. It was survival in a countryside awakening to yet another day of awesome famine.

CHAPTER FIFTEEN

Escape

AFTER SOME TIME I sensed that I was being followed. I quickened my pace and almost stumbled over uneven ground in the uncultivated field. I slowed down, aware that the figure behind me was gaining ground. I assumed my normal pace, deciding to bluff it out if indeed I were being pursued.

I was. A voice called out to me, clearly and resonantly in the morning air, in Katie's familiar tones. "Wait for me, miss. Wait for me!"

I stopped. It was pointless to run. The heavy brocade gown hampered my movements, and to try to run would be absurd.

Katie came up to me, panting. "I thought I saw you, miss. Suddenly you were there, outside the keep. I didn't see you cross the pavement from the house. It was quite light, and I don't know how I missed seeing you."

I said nothing, conscious suddenly of a violent headache. Sharp lights were dancing in front of my eyes. My vision was impaired. I could see only half of Katie's person. Everything seemed cut down the middle. I could not succumb to physical weakness, caused no doubt by the long, airless tunnel and fear of what lay ahead. I continued to tramp over the wet grass, holding my skirts at ankle length.

Katie hurried beside me. "I suppose the master forgot to lock the door. Yes, miss, I know he went to see you last night. He was drunk. Not a pretty sight, was he, but then he's never a pretty sight."

"Have you quarreled with him?"

Katie shrugged. "It's hard to tell. He says now he wants to marry you. He's said that ever since he had you locked up in the tower room." She plucked at my sleeve. "He can't marry you, miss. You know that, don't you? He can't marry his stepdaughter."

"I have not the slightest interest in his idea of marriage," I said haughtily.

Katie giggled. "He's in his dotage. I'm glad you realize that, too. Also has a fearful temper. I wouldn't like to cross him. When I first came here, he was nothing more than an ordinary agent looking after the estate for the old countess. Now look at him."

"You seem to know a good deal about Balaleigh and its occupants."

"Mrs. Rundle goes on and on about everything, especially when she's in a mood. Now that you're gone and the master doesn't know where old Maillard is, he will be in a quandary." She began to laugh. "Serves him right. But you haven't told me, miss, where you're going."

"I'm taking to the roads."

"That means certain death." She pointed across the fields. "Do you see the workmen shoveling the earth?

They're getting an early start so that all the burying will be finished before the day begins. That's what happens with these mass graves. They collect the bodies from the roadside and bury them together in the fields. In the full light of day, all you see is newly dug earth. Take to the roads, miss, and you'll soon be part of a pauper's grave."

I shivered but said nothing. I shut my eyes and saw bright lights forming a sharp mosaic of blue, green and red.

Katie went on, "You haven't had much to eat, miss, and you're weaker than you think. You won't be able to stand up to bad times the way you used to. Fever and starvation will strike you. One is enough to hurry you off. With both, you haven't a chance."

I wished she would go. I was in no mood to listen to the all too apparent miseries of the poor. Suddenly, behind me, I heard horses' hooves and, to my delight, Richard's voice.

"The top of the morning to you, Hannah. What are you doing on the road at this hour?" He reined in beside us, and I was surprised to see that Lady Caroline was his riding companion.

I looked at them both, but my eyes would not focus. I saw only half of each of them.

Katie smirked. "Sir, we're going for a walk. Miss likes an early-morning walk, don't you, miss?"

Speechless, I stared at Richard and Lady Caroline. Now was the time to cry out loud for help and to be taken under their protection. But I said and did nothing. My mind had gone blank. I could not think.

Lady Caroline was staring at me in a peculiar fashion. I thought she must have some intuitive inkling of my condition, but her question dispelled that possibility. "Hannah, isn't that the countess's gown—the one she wore in the Bath chair when she came down from the tower? Yes, it is. I'd recognize it anywhere. Are you indulging in some kind of early-morning masquerade?"

Katie laughed with mirth, then curtsied quickly. "I beg your ladyship's pardon. It isn't for me to approve or disapprove when miss is in a dressing-up mood."

"Is that so?" Lady Caroline looked at her coldly.

Richard dismounted and came toward me, his face perplexed. "Wherever on earth have you been, Hannah?" Under his scrutiny I was conscious, for the first time, of the dishevelment of my gown.

Seeing his puzzlement Katie said, "It was raining when we started out."

Richard turned his back to her and regarded me carefully. "Do you always allow your maid to take the initiative, Hannah?"

I tried to speak but could not. Richard's face was fast disappearing. The bright lights were multiplying. He said, "They told me at Balaleigh that you'd gone away for a short time to see your old nanny. I trust, Hannah, that you will be with us this evening at dinner."

Quickly I turned my back to Katie and took a step toward him. I pulled the pendant locket over my head and thrust it into his hand. Casually, Richard put his hand in the pocket of his riding jacket and remounted.

As they cantered off, Lady Caroline said, "Hannah's obviously not well. She seems..."

"I'll look into the matter when I return to Balaleigh," Richard replied.

I thought that all was lost, but had I asserted myself and spoken out, would things have been different? Richard would have taken me back to Balaleigh and looked into things. Now, until he began his inquiries, I was free on the road—at least I would be when I got rid of Katie. The sun went in, and the sky grew overcast. Miraculously, the bright lights in my eyes disappeared, and my vision adjusted itself.

"What was that you gave to Mr. Richard?" Katie asked.

"Nothing that was any business of yours."

"It was the locket, wasn't it? I saw it glint in the sun."

"What of it?"

"You're foolish to put too much trust in Mr. Richard. He says one thing and means another—just like I told you before. He's supposed to have broken his betrothal with Lady Caroline, yet here she is, just back from London, and he's taking her for morning rides."

"I suppose he knows his own business best."

"He'll know his business well enough to hand the locket to the master. You've really done yourself no good. One consolation is that they'll think you stole it and no one else. Miss, don't you see? I want to help you. That's why I brought you the locket. I couldn't help you much before with Mrs. Rundle always watching, but now, for the first time, I'll be able to do something useful for you. Will you trust me, miss?"

Of course I did not trust her, but I merely said, "Perhaps it would be better if we parted and went our separate ways."

"Oh, no, miss. It might rain any minute. If we hurry, we'll escape a drenching."

We crossed a field and came to a forked section of the road where ragged men were wielding picks and shovels.

"A relief road," Katie said, "that leads to nowhere. The track we're taking is a shortcut, straight into the town."

I was unfamiliar with the surroundings and found, to my chagrin, that I had to rely on Katie. But the main street was similar to other main streets I knew. It wound past small shops and houses in a legendary attempt to lose any evil spirits that might be lurking nearby. We left the high street and went down a cobblestone pass that led us to a two-story brown brick building, square in structure with an additional wing at the front. It rose up, stark and grim, from the cobblestones.

"We'll go around the back," Katie said.

"What place is it?" I asked.

"A place of shelter. They'll help us if they're not overcrowded."

I stared at her, dumbfounded. "I'm not at all sure that I want to go in."

She glanced up at the sky. "It's beginning to rain. At least it will keep us dry."

"So you're coming, too."

"Not for long, miss. Only until the rain eases. I've got to get back. You said you'd trust me."

"I wasn't aware that I had."

"You must, miss. They'll heed me. They know me."
She knocked on a wooden door with a grill set at
speaking level. A voice spoke through the grill. I did
not catch the words or Katie's low reply.

The door creaked open and Katie stood aside. "It's
all right, miss. You go first." With a deft movement
she stood behind me and gave me a push. I stumbled
over the threshold. Then the door shut, and I was
staring back at Katie through the iron grill.

"You'll be all right now," she said, "for good and
all. I'm the only one who knows where you are. Now
that you've gone, the master will marry me—not you,
a nameless pauper. I'm the one who will be mistress of
Balaleigh. Aye, the spoils of Balaleigh will be mine!
What you don't know is that Mrs. Rundle and I have
our plans—and the master will have, too, once we're
married. Among the ragged we'll find someone who'll
do what Maillard did—impersonate the countess for
as long as we want. And now that you're inside, don't
think that you can escape. These people are friends of
mine. They won't let you out of here."

I was pushed rudely aside by a short, stout man
whose coarse voice railed me. "What's the meaning of
sneaking in through the back way? Better ones than
you are taking their turns outside at the front."

"I—I'm not sure where I am," I gasped.

"Not sure, are you? You won't be long in doubt.
Now get going. Follow me and no misbehavior. We
like women to be docile."

I followed him along a dark passage. I thought I
heard Katie's triumphant laugh reach me through the

grill, but I could not be sure. The passage reminded me of the tunnel, the chief difference being that it was dry and clean. The high Gothic windows, set narrowly together, let in little light. I might have stumbled had not the man bullied me along.

We reached the front of the building, where there was a large, empty waiting-hall with bare boards and no seats. I noticed that the windows, about six feet from the ground, had windowsills sloping downward, which made impromptu seating impossible. At a desk behind a grill sat a hook-nosed man with spectacles; his dark blue jacket had the appearance of a uniform. My guide spoke to him in a low voice.

"Not regular," the man replied. "Not regular at all. Sent down from the Big House, did you say?" He wet his index finger with his tongue and flicked the pages of his ledger. "We're full up. We can't take newcomers."

"This one you can," my guide said. "Annie May died this morning. Give her Annie May's name. No need to alter the records. Annie May just didn't die, that's all."

"My name is Hannah McCabe," I said. Although I was trembling with apprehension, my voice was clear.

"Not anymore, it isn't. Annie May is good enough for you. Get moving."

I was prodded in the back and felt a stab of pain. We passed a door marked Board of Guardians, and all too clearly I realized my fate. Under the name Annie May, I had been admitted to the workhouse.

CHAPTER SIXTEEN
Annie May

I WAS TAKEN to an anteroom in which a matron known as Mrs. Nicholls stripped me of my clothes. Tall, gaunt and sharp featured, she made a face as she threw the gray brocade gown, now grubby and frayed at the neckline, into a heap on the floor. She removed my petticoats and shift and bade me take off my under-drawers, shoes and stockings. While I stood before her, shivering, she picked up the gown and searched for pockets. I was thankful that I had passed the locket to Richard and not hidden it in the voluminous folds of the gown. After her search proved fruitless, she flung the gown aside, consulted her file and peered at me over her spectacles.

"Annie May, eh? Well, you're a better-fed Annie May than ever she was. Into the bath with you. We never know what lice you newcomers bring in here. Not just paddling, either. Sit you down and wash yourself, do you hear? Behind the ears and all." She bundled up my clothes and put them on a shelf.

Two old women, newly admitted, were standing naked around a huge tin bath, waiting their turn to submerge themselves. With Mrs. Nicholls otherwise occupied, they mumbled their reasons for coming to the workhouse. Emma, eighty-eight, had not wanted to be a burden to her family, nor did she wish to die alone. Mary, fifty-seven, had been hungry. A third woman, who I learned was named Alicia, was still partly submerged in the tub. Hip deep, she was splashing herself in luxury.

"In you go," Mrs. Nicholls said, giving me a sharp push in the back.

"I—I bathed this morning," I said.

"Another wash won't do you any harm."

Alicia giggled. "Don't want to come in with me, do you? Not that I blame you, but in a few months there'll be little difference between you and me. We ladies have all got to live—even here." She spat in the water and lifted one leg over the side of the bath.

I seized the towel on a wooden stool and rubbed my back vigorously.

"Finished?" Mrs. Nicholls asked, turning from Mary to me.

I nodded.

"She hasn't even been in!" Alicia screamed.

My teeth began to chatter. There was no fire, and the walls were solid brick.

"Put on Annie May's undergarments." Mrs. Nicholls handed me a shift, underdrawers and long black stockings, which I felt sure had not been washed. Hesitating to put them on, I held them against me. They were too small.

"She was a small girl," Mrs. Nicholls conceded, eyeing my proportions speculatively.

"Why not my own clothes?" I asked, nodding at the bundle on the shelf.

"It's against the regulations."

"I can't go about like this."

Reluctantly, she reached for the bundle and handed it to me. "For the time being only. Too many paupers are being admitted. You'd never have got here if Annie May hadn't died. The new uniforms haven't arrived. Wear your own clothes until they come."

Quickly, before she changed her mind, I donned my own undergarments and the heavy brocade gown. Alicia, in her drawers and shift, regarded me enviously. "Where did you get that?"

"My business," I said.

"They'll throw rotten food at you in the dining hall, dressed like that. We're honest paupers here, not receivers of stolen property." Her voice was belligerent, and her eyes flashed. "You're one of us now. Just you remember that."

Not wishing for a fight, which might involve bodily contact, I answered tartly, "I shouldn't imagine there would be too much food to throw about."

"Smart one, mum," Alicia said to Mrs. Nicholls. "Like to know why she's here."

Mrs. Nicholls produced some shears. "Stand still while I crop your hair."

I gasped with disbelief and clutched my hair, which had grown quite long during my sojourn at Balaleigh. "Surely you're not going to cut my hair?"

"Regulations. You won't even comb it if we don't help you along."

"My hair is always combed."

"No exceptions." I felt the cold touch of the shears on the back of my neck. "There you are." She gave me a handful of my hair. "Put it over there in the wooden bucket and follow me."

Alicia giggled. "You aren't no lady now without your hair. I told you you'd soon be one of us."

"In no time it will grow again," Emma whispered.

Ignoring Alicia's jibe and nodding at Emma, I followed Mrs. Nicholls down a long, dark passage to the day room. There a number of girls, about the same age as I, were standing aimlessly about. Their shapeless, waistless gowns, of a woolen material with blue vertical stripes on a dingy white background, reached to their ankles, revealing heavy hobnailed boots.

A voice asked cheekily, "Who's the duchess, matron?"

"Annie May. She's taken the place of the girl who died."

"Why isn't she in uniform?"

"They haven't arrived. Get moving, all of you. The gong is about to go."

With murmurings of "bread and cheese," the girls filed out the door and down a flight of wooden stairs to the dining hall. I followed. Inside were women and girls and children of all ages, from the aged and infirm to the young and active. Segregated from the male members of the house, we stood at wooden benches set up before long tables while the matron said grace. Supervisors put bread, cheese and a small slice of meat on individual plates in front of us. We drank water from tin mugs, and as no cutlery was provided, ate with our fingers.

Rose White, who sat next to me, was kind and friendly. She was about my age. After the meal she took me to the dormitory, which contained two rows of eight troughlike beds attached to the floor and wall, with bare boards running down the center of the room and separating the two rows. Overhead were wooden rafters decorated with ubiquitous texts.

Rose looked at me curiously. "What was your real name, Annie?"

"Hannah McCabe."

"You've lost that forever. There's no record now of who you really are except the one the clerk has about Annie May."

"Who was she?"

"A farm laborer."

"How did she die?"

"Of a miscarriage, brought on by herself." Rose's voice was matter-of-fact. "Not her fault, either, that she got that way. Now they lock the dormitory doors at night. Some of the men used to wander at night."

"Good grief!" I stared at her wordlessly.

She patted my arm. "It can't happen now—not to any of us. Annie wanted to go home when she was sure, but there wasn't any home there. They'd all been evicted and died. She was the only one left."

Tears sprang to my eyes. "Did you like her?"

"Yes. She was one of the girls going to Australia."

"Australia?"

"We're all going to Australia, to a place called Melbourne. Every girl in this dormitory is going— sixteen of us altogether. We're waiting for six of them to come back from the rounds. They should be here by the end of the month. Then off we go! You, too, now you're Annie May. First by coach to Dublin, then by packet steamer to Plymouth, where we get the big ship for Melbourne, Australia. Five hundred and sixty-four orphan girls, they say there are, from workhouses all over the country, chosen to make servants for the colonists and wives for their laborers.''

I looked at her thin figure with compassion. "Aren't you afraid?''

Rose shrugged. ''I'd be more afraid to stay here for the rest of my life.''

The girls came trudging into the dormitory, weighed down heavily by their boots. Some of them had just returned from the rounds. They regarded me speculatively, then turned to Rose.

''New, is she?''

Rose nodded.

''What's her name?''

''Annie May,'' Rose said.

''What?'' Curious, they clustered around me.

''I'm not Annie May,'' I protested.

''Who are you?''

''Mrs. Nicholls calls her Annie May,'' Rose said.

''Annie May wasn't well fed like her.''

''What's she wearing that thing for? Why can't she dress like us?''

''At least her hair's cropped.''

''Does she think she's going to Australia? We don't want her kind there.''

''Stop it, stop it!'' I cried, my hands over my ears. They seized me, unbuttoned my gown and pulled it over my head; then they staged a tug-of-war. The gown did not tear. They bundled it up and threw it in the air. The skirt untwined, and it floated down like a balloon onto the bare boards between the beds. I snatched up the gown and put it on quickly.

Mrs. Nicholls entered, and all the girls became silent. I learned that I was to be set to work as a scullery maid. I had the task of scrubbing the floor of the waiting hall. Armed with a pail of water, scrubbing brush and floor cloth, I made my way to the hall in the afternoon. Mrs. Nicholls stayed with me just long enough to make sure that I remained on my hands and knees to give the maximum amount of energy to the scrubbing. The long skirt of the countess's gown got in the way, and I was obliged to hitch it up around my waist with a piece of string that I found on the floor.

It was the monthly visiting day of the gentry of the town. Mrs. Sanders, the wife of the master of the workhouse, greeted them with effervescence. The higher their rank, the more she gushed.

I was scrubbing steadily down the hall, keeping my distance from the guests, when a coach stopped outside the main door. Peering out, I saw a liveried coachman help a young woman inside. She was dressed in a blue velvet gown and her small bonnet was tastefully adorned with silk flowers. She appeared agitated.

"The horse bolted," the coachman said to Mrs. Sanders, who advanced to hover over the visitor. "My lady is a little upset, but no harm done. She's used to horses, but what could she do in the coach with the horse shying at the curve in the street as though some evil spirit had progressed too far?"

"Good gracious me! Is there anything I can do for you, my lady?"

"A glass of water, please. I shall recover in a moment."

Mrs. Sanders beckoned to me. Wiping my hands on the rinsed-out floor cloth, I curtsied and ran down the passage to the kitchen, returning with a glass of water on a tray. As I handed it to the young woman, she raised her head, and from beneath the bonnet her blue eyes stared at me. I found myself looking into the face of Lady Caroline.

I felt numb. I made no movement. She took the glass, sipped some water and informed Mrs. Sanders that she felt better. She put the glass on the tray, scarcely glancing in my direction. I retreated slowly along the passage.

"Who is that girl?" I heard her ask Mrs. Sanders.

"Annie May."

"That gown...I've seen it somewhere before, but I can't think where."

Mrs. Sanders seized her opportunity. "There's never enough money for uniforms. The poor wretch wouldn't be wearing it if we had a sufficient supply."

I heard no more, and when I returned, Lady Caroline had recovered from the harassment of the bolting horse and was being led into the boardroom by the simpering Mrs. Sanders.

I finished the scrubbing and went upstairs to the day room, where the women congregated before supper. I sat down on a backless bench and tried to still my racing mind.

Had Lady Caroline recognized me? Ruefully, I knew that I must look different with cropped hair, but I had no way of knowing how different, since the workhouse boasted no looking glasses. Yet the heavy brocade gown had caught her attention. Would she remember that she had seen it at dawn that very day? And if she did, would she pass the information on to Richard? Would either of them initiate inquiries into my whereabouts? But if they did, it was unlikely they would succeed. They did not know that an assumed name had been forced upon me, hiding my true identity with a deadly finality. No record existed anywhere, least of all in the workhouse, that Annie May had died and that Hannah McCabe had taken her place and name. Soon the girl known as Annie May, who was wearing the gown of the countess of Balaleigh, would be on her way to Australia.

Was I destined to be lost in the Antipodes forever?

CHAPTER SEVENTEEN

Back from the Rounds

UNDER MRS. NICHOLLS, my duties were to scrub and clean the waiting hall and the guardian's boardroom at 11:00 a.m. each morning. When my work was finished, Mrs. Nicholls inspected it and as a disciplinary measure took pleasure in finding fault with my labors.

"You're a good-for-nothing lump of a girl," she said. "It's high time you got out of that gown. Once the uniforms come, you'll look like everyone else—a little worse, maybe—and you'll have no reason to give yourself airs."

I protested hotly. "I don't give myself airs!"

"That isn't what I've heard in the dormitory. I've told the girls it's the fault of the gown, so if you want their goodwill, you'll eat humble pie, especially when you get your uniform."

I began to dislike the brocaded gown. I tried to keep it clean, but the daily scrubbing of the floor did not help in this respect. I wondered what the countess of Balaleigh would have thought had she known of the destination of her gown on the back of her great-granddaughter.

It was a summer day in June. I thought of Richard and felt sad and lonely. What was the future of our love for each other?

My misery increased, and I was relieved when Mrs. Nicholls called me into her office. On the table were the new uniforms. They were of a coarse woolen material with blue vertical lines on an off-white background.

"Don't stand there," she snapped. "Get off that monstrosity of a gown and try on one of these—the largest, I should say, seeing you've got that well-fed look."

I picked up a uniform and held it against me. Then I took off the gown and put on the uniform. It fit.

"Well, that's something," Mrs. Nicholls said. "Hand me that thing you've just taken off." Before I could reply, she snatched the gown from me and began to fold it.

"What are you doing with that?" I cried.

"Gor blimey, Annie May, what do you think I'm doing with it? I'm getting rid of it. You don't think Lady Caroline Edly is paying to have it washed and ironed to wear herself, do you? Why she wants it, I don't know. After the way you've torn it to tatters, it's a wonder she wants it at all."

My heart lifted with hope and expectation. Lady Caroline had recognized me, after all, but she wanted to make sure that this was the gown that had belonged to the countess of Balaleigh. I felt like singing. Mrs. Nicholls must have noticed my elation, for she said, "At least you're one of us now—almost."

It seemed that now I was. I walked everywhere almost unnoticed. I was just another girl with dark, cropped hair, wearing the workhouse uniform. When I went to the dormitory after supper, no derisive remarks were hurled at me. The girls were too busy talking to notice my nondescript appearance.

I got into my bed and settled down to sleep. Mrs. Nicholls came, snuffed out the candle and locked the door before departing. In the darkness I heard a stealthy movement that seemed to come close to my bed. At first I took no notice; then a figure slipped into bed beside me and whispered, "My, miss, what have they done to you? You look shocking."

It was Katie, returned from Balaleigh in what was known in workhouse parlance as "back from the rounds."

I gasped with surprise tempered with dislike and resentment. All week, girls who were emigrating had been returning to the workhouse from the villages and farms where they had been loaned out as servants with respectable families.

In a flash I wondered if Katie were emigrating. If so, why? What had happened to her grandiose plans to marry the master and become mistress of Balaleigh?

"Talk softly," she said. "No one will hear. I saw you in the waiting hall when I returned. You didn't see me. You were busy scrubbing."

It took me some time to adjust to her unexpected presence. With her lips close to my ear, she whispered, "I'm real sorry, miss, for what I did, but how was I to know how things would turn out? I did what I thought best."

"What happened?" I whispered back. My animosity toward her lessened slightly, but Katie scarcely heeded me.

"When I got back to the house after leaving you in what I knew to be good hands—after all, you didn't starve, did you, and you weren't whipped—everything was very quiet. There was no one about, and I wondered where they had all gone. Then Mrs. Rundle came to the front door, wringing her hands. She had seen me cross the pavement and wanted to know where you were. I told her I'd seen you come out of the old keep early in the morning and taken you to the workhouse. I knew Annie May, and that she'd just died. She was going to Australia, and I knew the workhouse wouldn't want to go to the trouble of altering the records."

I tried to move away from her, but she went on in a monologue. "Mrs. Rundle and I went inside the house and found the master lying at the bottom of the crumbling tower stairs. He was dead."

"Dead!" I interjected.

"Died of a stroke, the doctor said later. Apparently he'd been up to the tower room. It was too much for him. It was just as well he did die then. He had heavy gambling debts which could have caused him acute embarrassment. That's why he got us to do the inventory. To sell what he had was better than a debtors' prison, and that's what he had in mind. Well, there he was, dead, and you were gone, and no one at Balaleigh had any right to be there anymore. Mrs. Rundle said we'd all have to go. Mrs. Scott-Ryan went into hysterics, and Mr. Richard and Lady Caroline came and took control of things. I avoided them. I didn't want them asking questions about you after they saw us together that morning.

"I told Mrs. Rundle about that. She said they were asking for us both. She gave me some money and sent me off at once to her sister in Dublin. She said she'd meet me there, and she arrived some time later. She had told Lady Caroline that she didn't know about me but that you were always a little strange and had taken to the roads. Mr. Richard, beside himself, organized a search party. It went on for days, but no one knew anything. Then Lady Caroline told them all to go. No wonder she's got that fox's tail around her hat, and no wonder Mr. Richard thought twice about marrying her. Then Mrs. Rundle told me that Mrs. Scott-Ryan had panicked. She had nowhere to go, and to spite everyone, she set fire to Balaleigh."

"What?" I cried out, forgetful of the need for silence in the dormitory.

"Burned it down," Katie whispered. "All of it that would burn, anyway. They couldn't stop the fire once she'd got it going. She used the furnace to start it off. That's about the only thing she ever did efficiently in her life. The house burned for a long time. Now it's just a shell, like the old keep. The master's body got burned with it. It was like a kind of funeral pyre."

I was numb. The shock of Katie's disclosures made me completely devoid of feeling.

"What of Mr. Richard—and Lady Caroline?"

"They went to Matten. If Mr. Richard is still looking for you, he won't find you, because you'll be gone." Katie clicked her tongue. "I didn't want to stay in Dublin with Mrs. Rundle, so I ran away and used some money I had to get back to the workhouse. Here I am," she gloated, "just as though I'm returning from the rounds. We're both in the same boat, you know. We've got to make our own way in the world. That's Australia, where we're both going."

She slipped stealthily away and moved like a shadow to another bed.

By mutual consent, Katie and I avoided each other the next day. All the girls had now returned from the rounds, and we were told that we might depart any time now on the first stage of our journey.

My mind was in a state of constant confusion. I was not anxious to go to Australia, I did not want to remain in the workhouse, and I could not return to Balaleigh.

The following day each of us received six shifts, two red flannel petticoats, six pairs of stockings, two pairs of shoes and two gowns, one of which was made of a warm material. These had been provided by the parish, which also paid half our expenses. The other half was paid by the British government across the sea.

"Why are they going to all this trouble and expense?" Rose White asked Mrs. Nicholls.

"The colony needs domestic servants, that's why," Mrs. Nicholls snapped back at her. "If you don't give satisfaction, you'll be one of the first sent back."

It seemed as though my world had come to an end. I would never see Richard again or Lady Caroline or what was left of Balaleigh. I felt as if I were about to leave the face of the earth. The girls around me were quiet, and I wondered, with sudden compassion, if their feelings were the same as mine.

CHAPTER EIGHTEEN

Rescue

WHILE WE WAITED for definite word of departure from the workhouse, our daily tasks continued as usual. At eleven o'clock the next morning I was scrubbing the hall floor. Two workmen in blue smocks had a ladder straddled across the footpath to test the framework of the rear window.

The clerk dozed behind the grill of the inquiry desk. Mrs. Nicholls went once or twice into the board-room, where a meeting was in progress, then disappeared down the passage and did not return. The hall was empty.

A workman with his cap pulled over his face tapped on the windowpane to attract my attention. He pointed to the inside lock, and to oblige him, I crossed the hall and opened the window. As I did so, he pushed the cap to the back of his head. Much to my amazement, I found myself looking at Richard Ralston.

He put his finger over his lips, removed it and said loudly, "Thank you, miss." Taking some nails from his pocket, he hammered them lightly at intervals along the windowsill.

"Lady Caroline," he murmured, "is addressing the guardians in the boardroom on welfare work. Stop what you're doing and walk out the front door and turn to the left. The clerk has been well bribed. No one will deter you." Richard disappeared abruptly down the ladder.

Dazed, I picked up the pail of water and walked across the hall. I passed the clerk, who was sitting with his back to the door, his feet on a nearby table, snoring softly. I reached the door as one of the guardians entered hurriedly. He frowned at the ladders. I slipped to my knees and went on scrubbing.

"What are you doing there?" he shouted at the workmen.

"Mending the locks, sir," Richard replied.

"Who gave you permission to do that?"

"Isn't this number 7?"

"It is not. It is the workhouse."

"Sorry, guv'nor. We've come to the wrong place."

"I should think so. With all the expense we're under at present, we don't need to renovate windows that are never used. Be off with you."

The guardian thumped across the hall while Richard and his companion disappeared. From the corner of my eye I saw that the clerk had straightened himself and was busy with his ledger. I went on scrubbing, trembling violently but trying to appear calm. I heard the guardian open the boardroom door and shut it behind him. The clerk turned his back and put his feet up on the table again. Soon he was snoring.

I carried the bucket to the front door and got down on my knees as if to scrub the doorstep. I put the scrubbing brush in the pail, stood up and walked outside. As I went along the footpath to the left and around the curve in the street, I was almost praying that the evil spirits would not awaken to resume their capers in the daylight.

Once out of sight of the workhouse, I quickened my pace and was about to break into a run when I saw a coach waiting at the curb with the coachman in the box. The door opened and Richard, the workman's smock discarded, held out his arms. I almost fell into them. As he helped me onto the seat, he murmured, "My sweet, my lovely Hannah." The coach moved forward. Soon we were progressing at a rapid pace, not toward Balaleigh but along the road to Matten.

When I was sufficiently recovered, I gasped, "I never thought I would be rescued like this!"

Richard put his arm about my waist. "Lady Caroline tried to get you out to Matten on the rounds. They wouldn't allow it, even though they're indebted to her advice on workhouse management. They said Annie May was committed to go to Australia. Apparently the workhouses get certain advantages from the government by providing the colonies with orphans for domestic service."

The sound of his voice and his arm about my waist reassured me. "Am I safe now?"

"Perfectly safe—not as Hannah McCabe but as the countess of Balaleigh. Yes, my darling, I found the papers inside the locket."

"I'm so glad," I murmured. "They could have been so easily lost. But surely Katie didn't tell you where I was." My voice registered surprise and anger.

"Not Katie. She was too busy looking after herself. After she got back to Balaleigh that morning when Lady Caroline and I saw you both, the master had had a stroke and died. Katie disappeared, and Mrs. Rundle got out as soon as she could. Balaleigh was no longer any use to them or to Mrs. Scott-Ryan or Philip or Eton, who are both going into the civil service. None had any legitimate right to be there."

"But that still doesn't explain how you knew where I was."

"Do you remember when Lady Caroline and I saw you and Katie?"

I sat upright and looked at him accusingly. "Why were you with Lady Caroline when you said your betrothal was broken?"

"Touché." He squeezed my hand, then raised it to his lips and kissed it. "Lady Caroline and I are childhood friends, as you know. What is more natural than an early-morning canter? Now that I have found you, it is you and I who will canter across the fields." But his eyes continued to tease me, and overwrought, I put my face in my hands.

"Shall I continue?" he asked, concern in his voice.

"Please do. I must know."

"When we reined in and spoke to you, Lady Caroline thought you acted strangely and were dressed in a very peculiar fashion. And then she remembered it was the gown Maillard had worn when he came down from the tower in the Bath chair. We went back to Balaleigh to make further inquiries about you. When we got there, everyone was distraught about the master's death. Lady Caroline asked if you and Katie had returned. Mrs. Rundle said you'd taken to the roads. You'd acted so strangely, we thought that might be the case. We couldn't ask Katie if this were so, because Mrs. Rundle said she didn't know where Katie was. Mrs. Scott-Ryan knew nothing, so we organized a search party, which was of no avail."

"You said that morning they told you I was visiting my nanny. You knew I was never in a position to have a nanny."

"I did indeed, my pet. Lady Caroline and I were relieved to see you that morning but were worried about your strange behavior and appearance—and the fact that we couldn't find you after Mrs. Rundle said you'd taken to the roads. Then Lady Caroline went to the workhouse that afternoon and thought she saw you—with your hair cropped." His hand moved to tug playfully at my hair. "You've no idea how becoming it is," he murmured, replacing his arm about my waist.

"What happened next?" I whispered.

"Ah, yes...Lady Caroline made inquiries, but no girl with the name Hannah McCabe was in the workhouse. Well, Lady Caroline is nothing if not persistent. She went back almost every day, on the pretext of seeing if any girls were due to go on the rounds. She never saw you again."

"They made me scrub the hall in the mornings and not the afternoons."

"So that was it. Lady Caroline discovered that sixteen girls were leaving as domestic servants for Melbourne, Australia, including one girl who had never been on the rounds. This girl, now known as Annie May, had taken the place of the Annie May who had died. She believed this girl to be you. By devious means we found out that Annie May always scrubbed the waiting hall about eleven o'clock in the morning. Using her prerogative as a nurse and social worker, Lady Caroline asked to address the board of guardians on workhouse management this morning. In that way she knew that all the important people would be in one place, listening to her." He chuckled. "You know the rest."

"I do indeed." But I knew that I had to know more. "What about Balaleigh?"

"The house is almost as much a ruin as the old keep. Apparently, Mrs. Scott-Ryan, not wishing to leave what she couldn't have herself, set it alight—aided and abetted by Philip and Eton, who were at home from Cambridge during the long June vacation."

"Where has she gone?"

"To join Mrs. Rundle in Dublin." Richard's eyes were quizzical. "How did you get into the workhouse in the first place, my pet?"

I seemed to see Katie badgering the porter to let me in. I saw her gloating face through the grill when the door had shut behind me. I felt her lips against my ear and heard her voice whispering on. I hunched my shoulders and said, "It was the obvious place to go."

We sat in silence, but as the coach turned into the driveway of Matten, Richard withdrew from his pocket the oblong locket of the countess of Balaleigh and clasped it about my neck. With his lips on mine, he murmured, "For the present countess of Balaleigh."

I leaned against him with my head on his shoulder, knowing that with him beside me, my worries were over.

The nightmare of the workhouse was behind me.

CHAPTER NINETEEN

The Flowering of the Furze

LADY CAROLINE was kindness itself, and I soon recovered from my ordeal.

As soon as Richard knew this, he left for Cork to bring old Maillard to Matten. A few occasional remarks suggested that he took it for granted that the three of us were going to Australia. But despite his solicitude on my account, he had made no reference to our betrothal.

I was able to give Lady Caroline useful information about the workhouse. From her, I learned that the old countess had feuded with Lord Fullington, my father, over land and refused to recognize the marriage between him and her granddaughter. Shortly after the wedding, my father had died in a buggy accident abroad. When my mother had come home to have their child, the countess refused to accept my legitimacy. She had noised it abroad that the waiting woman had given birth to a child in her granddaughter's dressing room. Then she manipulated Lady Berenice into marriage with Scott-Ryan, an agent on the estate. When Lady Berenice died some years later, the countess farmed me out to the waiting woman, Anna McCabe.

"The old countess was an autocrat," Lady Caroline said. "She caused a good deal of misery in her lifetime, but now, thanks to Anna McCabe's loyalty in taking matters into her own hands and giving you the locket, all's well that ends well." She paused. "Did you ever hear what happened to her, Hannah?"

I shook my head. "Indeed, no. She and the children may have reached Donegal. They may be in a workhouse or—or a mass grave." I averted my gaze and wiped away the tears that had sprung to my eyes. I was sure then that Anna McCabe had known the sensual nature of Scott-Ryan when, on the roadside, she had warned me to be prudent. At her wits' end in the face of disaster, she had schemed my return to Balaleigh in the hope that somehow, with the help of the locket, I would find my rightful place.

When Richard returned with his grandfather, there was much talk concerning the old man's future. Maillard did not want to go to Australia. He wished to remain in the hills that had been his home when duties in the Balaleigh tower had not been pressing. But Balaleigh was gone, and the fiction of the old countess was gone with it.

"Why can't he stay here in the ruins of Balaleigh?" I asked, warmed to sudden inspiration. "He's used to puttering around the house. Why not leave him there with old Dan, to look after the place until the famine ends and it's rebuilt?"

The matter was settled. With the charm of the aristocrat that he rightfully was, Maillard accepted the post of caretaker in conjunction with Dan, who was as pleased to accept as Maillard.

"We'll keep the fire burning, in what is left of the old hall," Dan said with a knowing wink. "If it goes out, I'll know that something has happened to the mistress, but the Lord be praised, I hope I'll never see it."

When Richard took me to view the ruins of Bala-leigh, emotion filled my being at the loss of the old house.

"We'll have a home in each hemisphere," he assured me, squeezing my hand. "When the famine is over, this land will make good pasturage. Hundreds of sheep will graze here, and Balaleigh will be restored with the new countess in residence. You're still the countess, you know, even though we're going to Australia."

"Australia?"

His eyes twinkled as he chucked my chin. "Where sleepy little gray koalas nestle in hollows of eucalyptus trees and eat gum leaves, and red kangaroos jump on two legs over endless acres of grazing land. I love you, Hannah. I've loved you ever since I saw you waiting on the roadside with your foster mother and looking for all the world as though you'd lost everything that was worthwhile."

"I thought I had," I murmured. I raised my eyes to his. "Will I like it—this land you talk so much about?"

"Australia is a challenge, my love. If you can meet the challenge, it will accept you—and eventually love you. If not—" He shook his head.

"I'd always have Balaleigh to come back to."

"I want my wife to be with me—always." He kissed me.

"What about the practical difficulties of looking after two estates in two hemispheres?"

"We'll have two sons—one to inherit Balaleigh, the other to see to our Australian acres. What do you say, my darling?"

In answer, I put my arms around his neck and kissed him.

He held me close. "Do you see the yellow furze on the hills, glowing in the sunlight?" His lips were on mine. "If the furze flowers twice, kissing has gone out of fashion."

"It never flowers twice," I whispered, my mouth responding to his.

"Then kissing will never go out of fashion. Will you marry me, my precious?"

He bent his head to catch my reply and then gathered me into his arms with a great whoop of joy.

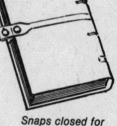